Happy Memories

Audrey Weigh

BOLINDA PRESS

Haunting Memories

Audrey Weigh

First published in 1974 by
Robert Hale & Company

Copyright © Audrey Weigh 1974

This edition is published in 1991 by
Australian Large Print
Melbourne, Australia
with the permission of
Robert Hale Limited

Cased   ISBN 1 – 86340 – 306 – X
Soft Cover   ISBN 1 – 86340 – 307 – 8

Typeset in 16pt Dutch by
Australian Large Print
Melbourne, Australia

Made & printed in Australia by
Griffin Press Limited,
Adelaide, South Australia

CHAPTER ONE

"IT'S JUST ridiculous," Jean Barnett insisted. She lifted the teapot, waved it absent-mindedly, then set it down again without even starting to fill the cups. "Whatever did you get such an idea?"

Elizabeth Gaunt smiled and gave a slight shrug. "I saw the advertisement in the paper," she repeated.

"I know that," retorted Jean. "What I meant was what on earth gave you the idea that it was suitable for you?"

"Well…" Elizabeth spread her hands helplessly.

"It's so isolated out there. You can't possibly imagine it when you've never seen the outback. Hundreds of miles to the nearest shop. No theatres, no neighbours. People don't live in places like that. They just exist — and vegetate."

Elizabeth's only answer was a weak smile. She knew there was no hope of making Jean understand why a remote area attracted her so much. It was the thought of isolation that had appealed to her when she first noticed the advertisement.

"Anyway, a governess job is not for you," persisted Jean."You're a fully-fledged teacher. And they're crying out for good teachers right here in

1

Adelaide. You'd be wasted up there." She poured the tea at last and handed a cup to Elizabeth. "Don't get carried away with rosy visions of an easy life," she went on. "I've heard about those sheep stations. The so-called governess ends up by doing the laundry, the washing-up and all the rest of the housework."

"It's not a sheep station," demurred Elizabeth. "It's a tourist resort."

"Same thing. They lure people up there with tales of a casual family atmosphere and a few hours schooling each day, then gradually push extra work onto them."

"Nobody's offered me the job yet," exclaimed Elizabeth. "And even if they do, it doesn't mean to say I have to accept. I might not like the people when I meet them."

Elizabeth's attention strayed from Jean's steady prattle. She should have kept the matter to herself until after the interview at least, but somehow her sister-in-law always managed to worm confidences from her. The arrival of a letter posted in Central Australia had brought the inevitable question about who she knew there, and since then Jean had fussed like a hen with her first batch of chickens.

An unexpected silence roused Elizabeth from her thoughts and she blinked in confusion.

"Well?" demanded Jean.

"Well, what? I'm sorry, I was thinking of something else just then."

"I said aren't you happy here?"

"Of course I am."

"What's the matter then? Why do you want to leave so suddenly and dash off into the back of beyond?"

"It isn't sudden," answered Elizabeth. She sipped her tea to give herself time to frame an explanation. "You and Bob have been very kind, having me here and looking after me, but I have to start out on my own again sometime. That advertisement seemed just right. A nice quiet place with accommodation and everything supplied."

"Those quiet places are the hardest to get away from. You'll be stuck there."

"I haven't done anything about it yet, except to write a letter," Elizabeth reminded her.

"But you're going to that interview."

"Yes, I'm going to meet the people at least."

A telephone call saved Elizabeth from further questioning and the conversation changed to the problems of a friend's baby, but when Bob arrived home from work the subject of Elizabeth's letter was raised again. He had less to say than Jean, but he also objected to his sister's plan.

"The climate will be too tough for you," he told her. "You haven't been through a typical Australian summer yet. This year has been much cooler than usual, and people up there would consider it winter weather in comparison to their summer temperature."

Their determination to put her off only increased

Elizabeth's enthusiasm during the following two weeks, but when the day of the interview arrived she felt stabs of doubt. She was to meet her prospective employer in a private room at one of the large city hotels. Surely it would only be a waste of time for them both? Jean and Bob were right. She was new to Australia. Too new even to think of settling in the centre of the continent. The Dead Centre they called it. A vast area of hot sandy wastes and dead vegetation. As Jean had said, the whole idea was idiotic.

Jean's final effort to dissuade her stiffened Elizabeth's resolve at the last minute. She chose a simple blue cotton dress with short sleeves that was her favourite and always looked crisp and neat. White sling-back shoes and a white handbag completed the outfit. Elizabeth smiled at herself as she gave a final pat to her hair. All this fuss to keep an appointment about a job that she was going to refuse anyway.

She rode into the city by bus, thinking it was a shame that crowds blocked out the view and turned travel into a nightmare during business rush hours. Adelaide was such a beautiful place. She should have found it easy to settle down and adapt to the way of life here. Compared with London or Birmingham it was very quiet and sedate, but the traffic still terrified her, even after three months.

The hotel receptionist nodded efficiently when Elizabeth approached the desk and spoke shyly to her.

"Mr. Hampton? Yes, he's expecting you. I'll tell him you're here." She swivelled her chair to face the small switchboard, flicked a switch and lifted a telephone receiver. "Miss Gaunt is here, sir."

For a few seconds Elizabeth studied the other woman, envying her for her poise. There had been a time when she had been confident and able to converse on equal terms with anybody.

"Mr. Hampton will see you now. Take the lift to the first floor and turn left. Room number one one six."

She wafted a hand in the direction of the lift and Elizabeth moved to obey, then stopped short. She hated lifts and if she stepped inside her last hope of arriving in a reasonably calm frame of mind would vanish.

"The first floor," prompted the receptionist.

Elizabeth could not bring herself to insist on using the stairs. "Thank you," she murmured, and stepped forward into the waiting compartment.

Mark Hampton leaned back in his chair at the sound of a hesitant knock on the door. This would be the fifth. No wonder the agencies always pleaded the difficulty of finding suitable staff when he complained about the girls they sent. Judging by the length of time it had taken this one to find the right room she must be a worse moron than the others.

"Come in," he called.

The door opened and Mark's eyes widened with

interest as a slender young woman entered. She closed the door and remained standing beside it, clasping a handbag tightly in her left hand. This applicant was completely different from the others; a single glance told him that. But she looked like a timid foal that would flee at an unexpected noise. He rose to his feet slowly and gazed at her for a moment, admiring the silver hair that waved softly around her face. As she made no move he beckoned her forward.

"Come in and take a seat."

"Thank you." Elizabeth crossed the room, but instead of taking the chair he pushed forward she stood rigidly in front of the desk. She looked at him, then down at the handbag that was now clenched in both hands, and her words tumbled out.

"I'm sorry, Mr. Hampton, but I shouldn't have come. It was all a mistake. I mustn't waste your time."

"Now wait a minute." Mark felt an urge to reach out and pat her arm, but he realised instinctively that the action would have the wrong effect. "Don't rush away just yet," he said. "I was just about to have a cup of tea. Surely you can spare five minutes to have one with me." He smiled at her in the way that appealed to all the lady tourists and she blushed faintly.

"Thank you. I would like some tea."

"Nothing stronger?"

"Stronger?" A flicker of revulsion crossed her

face. "Oh, no thank you."

As he leaned over to reach the telephone on the desk she sat down at last and he felt that he had gained some kind of victory. He had never met anybody quite like her before — so pale and slightly built, even frail looking. No doubt she was right, the job wasn't for her — she wasn't strong enough — but in the meantime he could enjoy her company.

Elizabeth watched him while pretending to examine the room. He was nothing like the man she had expected to meet. During the past fortnight she had read three books about the Australian bush, and all the photographs showed men who were large, unshaven and dishevelled; hats pushed to the back of untidy heads, cigarettes dangling from slack lips. Mr. Hampton was tall, over six feet she guessed, and he was broad, but apart from the suntan he looked like any city gentleman. He had grey eyes and light brown hair with a wide blond streak across the front. Nothing rough or shaggy about him. He turned to face her and she looked away quickly.

"Tea won't be long," he announced. "Now then, what shall we talk about?"

"Anything you like," she answered.

"Tell me about yourself."

"There's nothing much to tell."

"There must be. You have an interesting accent. English of course. How long have you been in Australia?"

"About three months."

7

"Long enough to decide whether you like it or not," he said. "Have you seen much yet?"

"Not a great deal. Only Adelaide and the Mount Lofty Ranges."

The arrival of a tea tray interrupted the stilted conversation and enabled Mark to suggest a move to more comfortable chairs near the window.

"I don't feel my usual self sitting behind a desk," he said. "But it did make interviewing easier. I've never tackled that job before and I was certainly glad the hotel manager suggested using this room."

He hooked one foot around the leg of a low table and dragged it into position near his armchair, then arranged the cups and saucers. "Black or white?" he asked.

"Oh, er, white please." Elizabeth supposed that if coffee could be described as white it was logical to use the same wording for tea, but the phrase still sounded strange to her ears. "No sugar please."

He handed a cup to her, then poured one for himself without milk and stirred in five lumps of sugar. "These biscuits don't look very exciting, but help me to eat them."

They munched biscuits in silence for a moment and Mark admired his visitor again. He had not met anybody so reserved and ladylike for a long time and the change attracted him. That silvery grey hair was eye-catching, too. Must be the new rinse in the city. It was unusual for someone of her age to apply for a job as governess. She must be in her late twenties or early thirties he guessed. All the others had been mere teenagers. He helped himself to another biscuit and pondered over his next remark. So far he had done nothing but ask questions. Perhaps he ought to talk about himself for a while.

"Some people wonder why I stay on the ranch so much," he said. "But I don't like Adelaide — or any city come to that. I go into Alice Springs every now and again, and I come down here once a year, but I'm always happier in the bush. No traffic problems, no rushing about, no need to lock anything up. The children like it out there, too. They're all good riders, of course."

He felt in his pocket for a wallet and flipped it open. "These are the kids. The youngest is Pauline. She's just five and ready to start school. Margaret is eleven now and in Grade Six. The others come in between."

Elizabeth took the black and white photograph and saw a group of five fair-haired children, all remarkably alike and all liberally freckled.

"They look very nice," she murmured.

"Yes, they're good kids. The trouble is, if I don't find a good governess I shall have to send them away to boarding school. The rest of us are too involved with tourists to pay proper attention to their education."

Elizabeth handed the snapshot back and he glanced at it briefly then sighed and returned it to its place.

"Tell me about yourself," he prompted. "You're a qualified teacher, aren't you? What brought you to Australia?"

Elizabeth stared at her hands for a moment then met his gaze again. "I was ill," she answered. "An accident... Then I was ill. I only had my brother and he was out here."

"So he suggested that you came out."

"Yes. I was only going to stay with Bob and Jean a little while, but I wasn't as well as I'd thought." Elizabeth looked down at her hands again. How could she explain the agonies she had gone through, trying to establish a new life for herself? Nobody could begin to understand the horror that she felt every time she had to mount a crowded bus or make her way along a busy street. Even the children at school had been too much for her. Facing a class of forty-six children had been commonplace once, but now she could not control half that number. On her very first day in an Australian class they had sensed her nervousness and become more and more unruly as the hours passed. Only half the week had elapsed before she gave up and reported sick.

Elizabeth gave a wry smile and her hands gripped together more firmly. That was the only secret she had managed to keep from Jean, the number of jobs she had turned down. Enrolled as a relief teacher she could have worked steadily throughout the term, but she had never managed more than a few assignments of two or three consecutive days. Bob and Jean had

10

assumed that the demand for relief teachers had slackened and never questioned the number of days she had spent at home, but her conscience would not permit her to impose on them any longer.

Looking up once more she found sympathetic eyes regarding her. He seemed about to speak and she lowered her eyes again quickly. What could she do about her predicament? She must get away from Bob's home and pull herself together. The advertisement had seemed to be an answer to her needs, yet here she was spurning the opportunity.

Mark crossed his legs and stared out of the window, not knowing how to bridge the uneasy pause. His visitor had obviously been through a terrifying experience and her sudden pallor and nervous twitching of her fingers showed that the memory was still overpowering. He felt impelled to help in some way, but his only assets were his business at the ranch. Gradually he began to picture her there. Surely the calm, easy-going atmosphere of the outback would be better for her than the rush of a city. They were isolated at the ranch, but the Flying Doctor Service would deal with any emergencies if she became ill again.

The prospect of seeing her relaxed and suntanned was attractive. Besides, he admitted to himself, he needed her. There were no other applicants to see and the other four had been useless. Maids and waitresses seemed difficult enough to hire at times, but finding a suitable governess was practically hopeless.

When he turned his head Elizabeth was still gazing at her hands so he was able to make a more leisurely survey. Now he could see the tip of a scar on the right side of her forehead, vanishing under the sweep of her hair, and patches on her forearms and the backs of her hands gave evidence of skin grafts. She looked up unexpectedly and he swept his hair back with an embarrassed gesture, hoping she had not noticed his curiosity.

"I must go now," she said softly.

CHAPTER TWO

" MISS — ER — Miss Gaunt, don't rush away."
Mark thrust out a hand to detain her and hastily
snatched it back. His arm waved awkwardly as he
tried to disguise his action, then he smoothed his hair
back again. "Look, Miss Gaunt, you must have
thought the post was suitable for you at one stage,
otherwise you wouldn't have answered the ad."

She responded with a barely discernible nod and
he leaned forward. "Why did you suddenly decide
not to go on with it? Was it anything to do with
seeing me?"

"No," replied Elizabeth quickly. "No, I made up
my mind before I ever came here."

"But you still came." He smiled gently, speaking
as he did when trying to soothe a frightened animal,
and she sank back into her chair. "Miss Gaunt,
you're exactly the kind of person I need for those
kids. They need someone to teach them other things
besides Maths and English. You'd be good for them.
You'd help them to improve their manners."

Elizabeth shook her head, but he pressed on.
"Miss Gaunt, you've no idea what kind of girls
they've sent me for governesses. Most of them were

just kids themselves. Some of them couldn't spell and most of them used bad language. I had to get rid of the last one because she drank too much."

"The poor children," murmured Elizabeth.

"Yes, they've had a raw deal. None of us wants them to be sent away, but things can't go on as they are." He pulled the snapshot out again and laid it on the arm of Elizabeth's chair. "They're too young to go away to school, aren't they?"

"Yes, it would be a pity to send them away from home."

"It would make everybody unhappy. I've even thought of giving up the ranch, and I've been there for twelve years now." His face brightened suddenly and he clicked his fingers. "Have you seen a pamphlet of Desert Oak Ranch?"

Before Elizabeth had time to answer he jumped up to fetch a brochure from the desk. He opened it out and spread it over Elizabeth's lap, then leaned on the back of her chair to point out a log cabin.

"That's the original accommodation. We only had four bedrooms, so most people had to camp out. I was everything then — tour guide, manager, even the cook — but things have changed now. I own the business and rent the land. It's part of a cattle station, you know."

Elizabeth stared at the brochure as he returned to his seat. The photographs showed well-spaced log cabins dotted amongst trees with straight, almost black trunks. A mountain range towered in the background, displaying a variety of colours from orange and red to blue and purple, and the small patches of grass around the buildings contrasted beautifully with the deep red of the soil. Horses were prominent in most of the pictures, Mr. Hampton riding at the head of small groups of tourists. She turned the page to find photographs of Aboriginal rock paintings and brilliant sunset scenes.

A quiver of excitement ran through Elizabeth as she looked at the brochure again. Desert Oak Ranch was far more picturesque than she had imagined. Jean and Bob couldn't have any idea what it was really like. How could they complain about her living in a place like this?

Mark noticed her interest and hope soared. Perhaps she would consider the post after all. He knew little about her, almost nothing in fact, but he could not resist feeling that she would be ideal for the children. He waited anxiously, not daring to speak in case he spoiled her present mood.

"I can understand why you became so fond of living there," she said at last. "The scenery is lovely."

"That's what all the tourists say." He leaned forward. "Miss Gaunt, wouldn't you like to see it?"

"Yes, but..."

"Say you'll take the job. Just try it. If you don't like it when you get there we'll let you come straight back again."

"That wouldn't be fair to the children."

"The children have had governesses coming and going so fast they lost count ages ago. One more won't do them any harm, especially when it's a chance to keep them at home. Say you'll give it a trial."

Elizabeth argued half-heartedly for a few minutes, mentioning her illness again and then her fear of crowds, but she only succeeded in convincing herself that she wanted to go. Mark had an adequate answer to all the points she raised, and he grinned broadly as he realised that he had won her over.

"We've got lots to talk about,"he told her. "Let's go out for lunch somewhere and decide what you need to bring with you." A flicker of apprehension crossed her face and he hastily amended his proposal. "We can have lunch downstairs and save going out. The food is quite good and it's much quieter than it would be in other places."

To Elizabeth's relief he ignored the lift and escorted her down the stairs to the ground floor. The drink waiter appeared as soon as they settled themselves at a table and Elizabeth asked for orange juice. Mark ordered beer for himself.

"Do you ever drink beer?" he asked.

"No," answered Elizabeth quickly. An expression of alarm flashed over her face, reminding him of her reaction when he had offered her a drink upstairs, and he held back his intended remark about how popular cold beer was in dry country. Once again he found himself wondering about the accident. What could have happened to cause a young woman such terror that she lost all her self-confidence and gave up a career? It was a sure bet she would never have considered moving to the bush before that event.

Elizabeth chose a light meal of tongue and salad, while her host ordered soup, fish, steak and apple pie.

"I see you don't eat much lunch."

"No, I never have."

"I don't usually have fish, except as a main course on Friday nights. It's a long way to transport it, just for an in-between dish. I never reckon I've had a full meal if I don't get soup, though."

Conversation was desultory, with long pauses while Mark enjoyed his food. Elizabeth began to relax in the easy-going atmosphere, and by the time coffee was served she felt composed enough to discuss her new job properly.

"The outback will do you the world of good," said Mark, counting out five lumps of sugar and stirring his coffee well. "Can you ride?"

"No. I've never been on a horse in my life."

"You'll soon learn. All ours are very placid. The fresh air will bring your strength back in no time."

"I'm going to work, not for a rest cure," laughed Elizabeth.

Mark smiled back. "It won't be hard. A trained teacher like you could do it with one arm tied behind her back and standing on her head as well."

He watched the glimmer of amusement in her

eyes and leaned forward. "No, seriously, it'll be easier than anything you've ever done before. The kids have correspondence lessons and School of the Air. All you have to do is supervise while they get on with it."

Elizabeth was appalled. "Do you mean they've been doing their work all by themselves?"

"Just about. Except when they get stuck, of course. Some of the girls seemed to find it hard explaining sometimes, but you won't find the job difficult at all. All the lessons are prepared by the Correspondence School, and they mark the papers as well."

"Do the children enjoy their work?" asked Elizabeth.

"Kids never do, do they? They like School of the Air, though. Hearing the other kids makes it more interesting, I suppose."

Although she said nothing her expression gave her away. Mark noted her disapproval and guessed what line her thoughts were taking. It all helped to convince him that she was the right person for his family.

"You'll do wonders for them," he declared. "You'll know how hard they should be working and answer all their questions. They'll improve in no time. They're sure to."

"What about books?"

"Those are all supplied by the schools. Now then, we've agreed that the work won't be any trouble.

The question is, how do you want to travel?"

Elizabeth looked up enquiringly and he made another awkward flourish with his hands. He did not want to cause any further fear or embarrassment by speaking about the accident, but he had to broach the subject of transportation somehow. The prospect of travelling all that way could make her change her mind even yet.

"Hm," he began. "Well, there's the train of course. People find that interesting and quite restful. Others prefer to fly. From Alice Springs we have the bus tour and regular flights." He took the plunge. "How do you feel about air travel?"

"I flew to Australia," answered Elizabeth. She knew what he was trying so hard not to mention and forced herself to speak lightly. "That accident happened in a boat."

"A boat?" exclaimed Mark involuntarily.

"A kind of ferry. In Greece. It was packed with people." Elizabeth saw the scene again in her mind; the overcrowded vessel, the fire and the screaming passengers. Crowds always brought that vivid picture back. Hastily she cast the memory away. This time she was going to succeed in making a new life. All that horror belonged in the past. She managed a shaky laugh. "I'm not likely to need a boat to get to the ranch, am I?"

Mark laughed with relief. "Not at all" he assured her. "You'll be lucky to see any water in the river at all. Even the regatta at Alice Springs is run in a dry

19

bed. They take out insurance in case rain comes and spoils everything by filling the river up."

They talked far more easily after that. Elizabeth decided to go by train so that she could see more of the countryside on her way to the Centre, then travel on the coach with the tourists on packaged holidays.

"I'll send you the ticket," he told her. "George will meet you in Alice and take you to a hotel for the night. He's our coach driver."

There seemed to be nothing else left for them to discuss. Elizabeth gathered her gloves and handbag, and Mark suddenly remembered to leap up and move the chair back for her. As they shook hands he noticed the scars again and worried about her decision. She could still change her mind, especially if her city friends started telling far-fetched tales.

"Don't let me down," he implored. "Promise you'll come. Those kids really need you."

"I'll come," she answered. "Thank you for that lovely lunch."

Preparations kept her busy for the next two weeks. Her brother had accepted the idea of her taking the new job and had even become slightly enthusiastic, but Jean worried incessantly about the heat and strong sun.

"There are snakes, too. And poisonous spiders."

The prospect of living in the midst of all the insects she heard about was not encouraging, but Elizabeth refused to surrender to Jean's pressure. Whenever she felt swayed by her sister-in-law's arguments, she thought of Mr. Hampton's last plea and her promise. She was needed up there. If she changed her mind those poor little children would be sent away from home and their lives would never be the same. It was a long time since she had felt needed anywhere and she must do her best, for her own sake as well as theirs.

Jean had not become sulky when her advice was rejected. She helped Elizabeth in any way she could and drove her to the railway station on the day of departure.

"Here's your seat. Your luggage will be sent right through to Alice so you won't have to bother any more about it," she said.

"Thank you, Jean. You've both been very good to me. I'm sorry if I've been a bit of a nuisance sometimes."

"Nonsense." Jean's eyelids were pink and she blinked rapidly as she spoke again. "We've enjoyed having you. Don't ever think that you were a nuisance."

"I'm very grateful. I'll never be able to tell you how much it meant to me, staying there with you and Bob."

Jean blinked again and caught hold of Elizabeth's hand. "Listen, Elizabeth, don't ever be afraid to come back. If you don't like it for any reason at all, come back right away. Don't stick it out just because you're proud or anything. We won't laugh at you if you decide that you made a mistake."

"Don't worry, I'll be the first to admit it if things don't work out right. You'd better go, Jean. It's nearly time."

Thank goodness Bob had gone off to work as usual. Saying good-bye to both of them at the station would have been an ordeal. Elizabeth felt her eyes grow misty again as the train picked up speed. Starting a new life in a different part of the country should be exciting, but at the moment she could think only of the comforts she had left behind. She clenched her fists and tried to plan for the future. During her illness she had often started crying for no apparent reason and then found it impossible to stop. She must not cry now. She was better and she was just about to begin a wonderful new existence.

Chapter Three

ELIZABETH REACHED Alice Springs after half past eleven on the second night. George met her at the station, a short, cheerful young man with a bulging waistline, and drove her to a hotel. In the morning he loaded his coach with supplies for Desert Oak Ranch and they set off into the countryside with a party of tourists.

The sealed road came to an end after a few miles, and as they bumped over rough surfaces Elizabeth realised why the coach looked so dilapidated. From then on the only sign of human habitation was a signpost directing travellers to a homestead, and George cooked a barbecue lunch for his passengers in a dry creek bed. He told Elizabeth that that the road became very sandy further along and he often had to dig the vehicle out. Elizabeth was enthralled by the harsh desert scenery, so different from anything she had ever seen before, but the heat and the long journey had tired her and she fell asleep during the afternoon despite the jolting.

She was aroused by George telling everyone that the ranch was in sight. He brought the coach to a halt outside the largest building, and before the dust had time to settle a door opened. Elizabeth recognised Mr. Hampton and felt a sudden stab of nervousness. He looked entirely different today in open-necked shirt and high-heeled riding boots, but even in casual clothes he carried an air of authority.

As he reached the door of the coach a large black dog bounded around the corner of the building, followed at a short distance by a red-haired puppy.

"Down," ordered Mark curtly.

The black dog immediately sat, and after a moment of indecision the puppy followed suit. Mark climbed into the coach and smiled a welcome to his tourists.

"I hope you all had a good journey," he said. "Just stay in your seats for a moment until you know which cabins you'll be in." He turned to Elizabeth and his smile became warmer. "I'm glad you came. Just go through there and you'll find yourself in the kitchen." He waved his hand towards a door next to the one from where he had emerged. "George will introduce you to everybody. I'll come and see you after I've got all the tourists settled."

Elizabeth collected her hat and basket from the rack and followed George into the kitchen. It was a square, spacious room which gave an instant impression of orderly routine. A small, thin woman was standing behind a long table, stirring batter with a wooden spoon. She eyed Elizabeth briefly, then turned her attention back to her work.

"This is Miss Gaunt," said George. "Elizabeth."

The woman merely nodded and George added, "This is Mrs. Annie Fenn, our cook."

"How do you do," murmured Elizabeth. The cook nodded again and Elizabeth felt a sudden flash of indignation at her unwelcoming attitude. After Mr. Hampton's enthusiasm about the ranch and his remarks about how sorry everybody would be if the children had to leave, she had hoped for a better reception than this. Even her mental picture of a professional cook had been wrong. She had imagined a large woman, perhaps running to fat, and far more talkative.

"Where's Noreen?" asked George.

"In the laundry. The generator broke down again today, so we've had no power most of the day. Don't know why they don't dump that old thing and get a decent one."

"I suppose Olive and Louise are down in the cabins then?"

"Yes, they're trying to get all the pillow slips on before the customers get in."

George looked around helplessly. "I've got to unload that coach. Where are the kids, anyway? They should be here."

"Knowing Margaret, she'll be miles away. No doubt the others too."

"I bet Carl and Pauline are somewhere around. They're too nosey to vanish at a time like this." George stalked to the back door and pulled it open. "Carl! Pauline! Where are you?"

The red puppy loped up to the door and George put his foot out to hold it back. "Not in here." He bent down to give it a friendly pat as it obeyed, then raised his voice again. "Come on, Carl."

A smothered giggle answered him, then two young children slid into the kitchen and stared at Elizabeth. She smiled and they both giggled again.

"This is Carl and Pauline," said George. "Here is your new teacher, Miss Gaunt."

"Hello," said Elizabeth.

"Hello," answered Carl.

Pauline covered her mouth with one hand, moved it momentarily to say"Hello," then clasped it over her mouth again to repress another giggle.

"They'll know where to take her," said Annie. "Let them get started now instead of holding everything up in here."

"Do you know which room Miss Gaunt is having?" asked George.

Carl nodded. "Number ten. That's because it's at the end."

"Well, you show Miss Gaunt the way. Your Dad will be along soon. I'm going to unload the coach." George propped opned the front door open with a stool and turned back to Elizabeth. "Sorry there's nobody much around to meet you at the moment. Things seem to be a bit chaotic, but we'll be sorted out soon. Carl and Pauline will look after you."

Determined to make a friendly start, Elizabeth smiled at Annie as she passed the table. There was no change in the woman's expression, but she spoke to George almost immediately afterwards. The door closed slowly and Elizabeth had no difficulty in hearing the testy remark.

"Can't see what she's got that entitles her to one of the tourists, cabins. We're short enough these days as it is."

Elizabeth had no time to dwell on the meaning of that, or the fact that she had not met with Annie Fenn's approval. As soon as they were outside Carl and Pauline seemed to lose their shyness.

"Can I carry your basket?" asked Pauline.

"No, I'll carry it," said Carl at once.

"I asked first."

Just a minute, laughed Elizabeth, as Pauline made a tentative grab for it. "I think boys should carry luggage. It's good practice for when they grow up."

Carl grinned triumphantly, but before Pauline could object Elizabeth added,"You can carry my hat for me if you like, Pauline. That's much more ladylike."

The little girl took the hat and ran her hand lightly over the crown, then turned it around to admire the bow at the back.

"This is pretty. I like it."

"Thank you."

"Your cabin is along here." Carl led the way along a red dirt path and the others followed. After a few steps Pauline skipped to Elizabeth's left side and took hold of her hand.

"We've been waiting and waiting for you to arrive," she said.

"You must have been glad to hear the coach then. Where are all your other brothers and sisters?"

"I've only got one other brother."

"Oh. Well, where is he, and your sisters?"

Pauline pursed her lips thoughtfully. "Brian will be with Margaret," she answered at last. "And Julie will have gone too."

"They must have got tired of waiting, I suppose."

Carl had stopped at a fork in the path and he turned to face them as he heard the last words.

"They weren't waiting," he informed her frankly. "Margaret said there wasn't much holiday left so they'd better not waste it."

"I see." Elizabeth forced a smile to cover her confusion.

"You can go two ways to your cabin from here." Carl swung the basket to indicate the diverging paths. "That one's quicker but it's steeper. That one goes round the back of the cabins."

"Well, let's try the quick way this time, shall we? Then I can see the front of everything."

Loose sand and small stones slithered under their feet as they descended the short hill, but it was not very steep and Elizabeth was able to look at the view as she went. Red sand dotted with sparse vegetation stretched towards a low mountain range. The sun was sinking rapidly, casting a rosy glow on protruding rocks and creating deep purple shadows in the crevices. Elizabeth gazed wistfully at the colours. If she could paint, what a beautiful picture that would make.

"This is number ten," said Pauline, bringing Elizabeth's attention back to immediate matters. "Dad put you in this one because it's the last one."

Elizabeth was reminded instantly of the cook's last remark, one that had not even been directed at her. It had seemed to imply that the new arrival had been specially favoured.

"Didn't your other governess sleep here?" she asked.

"Oh, no!" Pauline's tone clearly expressed her scorn. "She stayed in the main house. Dad chose this one specially for you because it's quiet. Nobody walks past much, you see."

"How nice of him to think of that," answered Elizabeth.

She could not think why the usual arrangements had been changed for her benefit, but she did not want the children to attach any importance to it so she said no more. Carl ushered her into the log cabin and she clasped her hands together with delight as she looked around.

Mr. Hampton had assured her that the accommodation would not be at all primitive, but she had prepared herself for something rather rough and ready. Nothing could have led her to expect a room like this, she thought. The log walls were beautifully varnished and two zig-zag patterned mats lay on the polished wood floor. A single bed stood against one wall under a window, and its cotton spread matched the cushion in a corner of the easy chair. There were two cupboards against the wall opposite the bed, and a table and upright chair near the centre of the room.

"This is your wardrobe," said Pauline, flinging open one of the cupboard doors. "That other one's got shelves in for the rest of your junk. I mean things."

"How nice."

"This is the bathroom," said Carl, determined to take a leading part in showing off her new abode.

"My goodness, this is big," gasped Elizabeth.

"You can hang your undies up to dry at this end," declared Pauline, pointing out a clothes line in the vacant space.

Elizabeth dutifully admired the gold coloured bath mat and the pink and yellow flowers decorating the shower curtain, then they returned to the bedroom. Carl demonstrated how to use the air conditioner, then they all looked at each other, uncertain what to do next.

"I'll go and get your luggage," said Carl.

"You won't be able to carry it, I'm afraid. It's much too heavy. George will bring it down when he's not so busy."

"I'll manage easily." Carl darted out of the door and Pauline immediately followed.

Elizabeth chuckled softly to herself and turned to

inspect her surroundings again. In contrast to the intense heat outside the air conditioner had kept the room pleasantly cool. The three outside walls each had a window and all the views were spectacular. Elizabeth tossed her handbag onto the bed and sank into the easy chair. She could enjoy living here, she was certain of that. Jean's worries and fears seemed ridiculous now. Her new life was going to be a success, and when they had had a little time to get acquainted, even Annie Fenn would be friendly. At the memory of the cook's cool reception Elizabeth frowned, but childish giggles distracted her from her thoughts. Obviously Carl and Pauline were on their way back.

Elizabeth went to the door and stopped short in surprise. The two children were pattering down the slope, holding back a large wheelbarrow that threatened to run away from them. In the barrow lay her red suitcase.

"I told you we could do it," boasted Carl, reaching the door and coming to a stop safely.

"So you did. Fancy thinking of using a wheelbarrow."

"We brought the red one because that's the one you'll probably want first," said Pauline. "George said you used it last night."

"That's right. Thank you very much."

Refusing any help, Carl struggled into the cabin with the suitcase. Elizabeth closed the door again to keep out the the heat, and picked up her handbag to look for the keys. She thought it seemed churlish to send the children away when they were so eager to help, but she knew it would embarrass her to unpack in front of them.

"How long are you staying?" asked Pauline.

"A long time, I hope."

"I hope so, too. You're much nicer than we expected."

Caught unawares by that candid statement, Elizabeth could make no response. Her fingers stopped for a moment, then she fumbled more rapidly and pulled out a bunch of small keys.

"We'd better go, else we'll be in trouble," said Carl. "See you later, Miss Gaunt. Dinner's at seven."

"Thank you." Elizabeth turned a key in the locks and smiled at the children as they went. She had never met any quite like them before, so grown-up in some ways yet so childishly outspoken. She was quite certain she would enjoy teaching them and finding out all their strange little habits. She raised the lid of the suitcase and started in consternation at the film of red dust beneath. Thank goodness Jean had warned her to cover the contents with a sheet of plastic. Her hands were filthy, too. She had better wash before touching any of her clothes.

Elizabeth hurried to the bathroom and as she reached the washbasin near the window she heard Pauline's voice outside.

"Margaret was all wrong about her, wasn't she?"

"Yeah."

"They'll be sorry now that they didn't stay and see her."

"Margaret won't. She said she's bound to be nice when she first gets here. It's after school starts that you have to watch out."

"Well, I like her and I hope she stays." There was a pause then Pauline's voice continued. "Mrs. Fenn doesn't like her. You could tell."

"Huh! Mrs. Fenn doesn't like anybody."

The chatter faded away as the children moved farther along the back path and Elizabeth turned on the tap to wash her hands. That was the second time Margaret's name had been mentioned in the same manner. It seemed that she was likely to prove something of a rebel. Elizabeth sighed as she replaced the towel on the rack and went back to start unpacking. Mrs. Fenn's hostility probably wouldn't matter very much, but it was to be hoped that Margaret would not prove to be too difficult.

Chapter Four

A SMART rap sounded on the door about ten minutes later. Elizabeth found Mark Hampton on the step, her other suitcase in his right hand. The black dog stood beside him, tongue lolling out and tail wagging slightly.

"I brought the rest of your gear down. How're you getting on?" said Mark.

"Oh, very well thank you." Elizabeth looked down at the dog. He was obviously friendly so she stretched out a hand to pat him. The dog moved forward to meet her hand, sniffed it and licked it gently. "He's a lovely dog," said Elizabeth, rubbing him behind the ears. "What's his name?"

"Bruce. Shall I bring your bag right inside?"

"Yes please." Elizabeth stepped aside and Mark strode into the cabin. Bruce sat down with a patient air to wait and Elizabeth gave him a final pat before entering again. Mark rested his hands on his hips and looked her over appraisingly.

"Well, the trip doesn't seem to have done you any harm."

"I'm very well, thank you. It's a long way, but I found the railway journey quite restful."

"I was relieved to see you on that bus this afternoon You've no idea how many people accept jobs up here, then back out because their friends tell them tall stories. Didn't anybody try to put you off?"

Elizabeth smiled and managed to answer lightly. "My sister-in-law seemed to think I would be in dire danger."

"What from?"

"Well, snakes for instance."

"Snakes!" he exploded. A strange expression flashed across his face, but vanished immediately. Surely not fear? Elizabeth told herself that was a ridiculous thing to imagine. It must have been impatience or scorn rather than fear. He was accustomed to the bush and all its wildlife.

Mark raised a grin. "City people!" he scoffed. "They always reckon to know all about the bush, especially those who've never been to experience it first hand. You'd be surprised at the outlandish stories we've heard. Break down in the bush and the first thing some tourists worry about is dingoes. They seem to think they lie in wait for marooned tourists and then attack like wolves." His grin widened. "Glad to see you paid no attention to anything they told you, anyway."

The blond streak of hair had fallen forward over his brow. He brushed it back then scanned the room as though to check that everything was in order.

"What about the others?"

"Well, as a matter of fact I haven't met them yet."

"You haven't? Weren't they waiting for you?"

Elizabeth faltered at the sharp tone. He was obviously displeased, but there was no point in trying to protect the children by evading the issue. "No, I didn't see them."

Mark strode to the door and flung it open. "Carl!" he shouted. "Carl! Tell the others to get here at once."

"They're at the stables, Dad," came a voice from the distance.

"Well, get on your bike and get down there fast. I'll give you five minutes. Make sure every one of you is here by then."

He paused on the doorstep, taking deep breaths to recover his poise, then returned to the cabin. "I'm sorry they weren't here to meet you. I hadn't realised their manners were that bad."

"Children are often slack about things like that — they get taken up with whatever they're doing at the time," answered Elizabeth, trying to smooth the affair over. This was hardly the way to begin a good relationship with her pupils. They would resent her from the start if their father were severe with them over their lapse this afternoon.

"They should know how to behave by now. The summer holiday is far too long. They've been running wild."

He stalked to the door again and stood on the path outside, staring grimly in the direction of the stables. Elizabeth sighed and continued tidying her belongings away. Not many minutes passed before she heard the scuffling of wheels braking on the path.

"Hello, Dad," said a meek voice.

"What's the meaning of this behaviour?"

"What behaviour?" asked another voice.

"You know perfectly well. Sneaking away to the stables when your new teacher was due to arrive. I'm ashamed of you. How do you think she felt, travelling all this way for your benefit, then finding you hadn't even got enough manners to be here? It would serve you right if she turned right round and went back again."

Sorry, Dad."

"I should think so, too. Now just remember what I told you. If you don't behave properly and work well this term, it's off to school for the whole lot of you. I'll have no more of this kind of nonsense."

Subdued apologies followed and soon afterwards Mark tapped on the door again. Elizabeth answered and found herself facing a row of five children, all standing in order of age with the eldest on the right. Each one had curly light auburn hair and abundant freckles. They eyed her uneasily, wriggling their bare feet in the red dirt. Even Carl and Pauline had taken their shoes off now, she noticed. They must have been wearing them specially to give her a good impression when she arrived.

"My children," said Mark. He pointed to each in turn. "Margaret, Brian, Carl, Julie and Pauline."

37

"Hello, Miss Gaunt," they chorused.

"Hello. Goodness me, aren't you alike? It's a good job you're all different ages, otherwise I'd get you all mixed up."

"They want to tell you they're sorry for not meeting you properly when the bus came in," said Mark. "Especially these three. They didn't even put clean clothes on."

Margaret tilted her chin a little and looked into Elizabeth eyes. "I'm sorry I wasn't ready to meet you."

"That's all right, Margaret. I'm sure you didn't mean to be rude."

"I'm sorry, too," said Brian, gazing steadfastly at the ground and scuffling one foot nervously.

"Sorry," whispered Julie.

"It's quite all right. I'm glad I've met you all and I hope we get on well together."

"The gong will go soon," said Mark. "You kids go and get cleaned up quickly."

The children scampered away, glad that the ordeal was over. Only Carl looked back and waved before mounting his bicycle.

Mark gazed thoughtfully at Elizabeth. "I've arranged for you to have dinner in the kitchen, Miss Gaunt. Do you mind?"

"Mind? Oh, no, of course not."

"I always have mine in the dining-room with the guests. You can eat your meals with the guests if you'd rather, but it does take rather a lot of time. I thought you'd have more time to yourself if you ate in the kitchen."

"It would be better that way I think," answered Elizabeth. "Especially when we start lessons." It occurred to her that her new employer was being exceptionally considerate about her privacy and time. "Excuse me asking," she said, "but why did you give me one of the tourists cabins instead of the usual governess's room?"

Mark was taken aback by her question. He hesitated for a moment, then shrugged his shoulders. "Well, as a matter of fact, I wanted to make sure you would stop here — if you ever actually arrived. I didn't think you were the type to enjoy life in the main house with the rest of the staff. Radios going and all that kind of thing. And you'd have to share a bathroom."

"Well, it's very good of you. I think this is lovely."

"I'm glad you like it. I want you to stay. You're the only person I've ever found who's really suitable for those kids."

His sincerity embarrassed Elizabeth and she tried to pass the moment off with a joking remark. "You don't really know that yet, Mr. Hampton. I haven't even started work."

"I'm sure of it." He bit his lip and frowned thoughtfully. "How did you know this wasn't the usual accommodation for a governess, anyway?"

"Well, as a matter of fact I guessed most of it. I

overheard someone talking."

"Annie Fenn," he declared. "Don't say anything else — I know it was her. Nobody can cause trouble like that woman. And I'm perfectly sure you didn't overhear whatever she said by chance. She'd make quite certain that you could hear before she started to say it." He shrugged again. "Take no notice. Nobody in the Territory can stand her ways, but she's a good cook and that's what matters. It's hard to get someone out here in the summer. We only have to put up with her till our regular gets back."

He escorted her as far as the kitchen, opened the door for her and poked his head inside. "Look after Miss Gaunt, George, and introduce her to everybody. She doesn't seem to have met many people yet."

Elizabeth entered shyly and looked about. Annie was busy at the stove and paid no attention, but two younger women stopped folding paper serviettes and stared at her with interest. George left a pile of cardboard cartons in the corner and came across to her. His shirt was dark with perspiration and it hung out at the back of his trousers.

"Just finishing unpacking all the stores," he told her. "Let me introduce you to the rest of the mob. This is Olive and Louise. They do the rooms and waitressing."

"There's no such word as waitressing," snapped Annie, turning around suddenly. "A waitress waits. People are much too casual with the English language nowadays. You should take more care especially now that we have a real teacher here." She glanced at Elizabeth as she spoke, derision plainly displayed. Elizabeth flushed and the cook's mouth curved slightly.

"Never mind about grammar and such," retorted George, apparently undisturbed by the interruption. "Elizabeth, this is Olive. She's been here almost a year. And this is Louise. She's been here since Christmas."

"How do you do," murmured Elizabeth.

"Glad to meet you," said Louise. "Do you think you'll like it here?"

"I hope so."

Olive merely nodded, looking intently at Elizabeth as though she were assessing her qualities, and George waved an arm towards the table where places had been set for six. "Take a seat, Elizabeth. Noreen and Charles'll be in to join you in a minute. I'll just stick those boxes in the cool-room, then grab a shower."

Elizabeth sat down at the table, choosing a chair which gave her a view of the room and its occupants. She noticed with surprise that Annie cooked on a large black range with a wood fire, although a modern gas stove stood beside it and an electric stove only a few feet away. Louise gathered up all the folded serviettes and carried them into the next room, smiling at Elizabeth as she passed. She was an attractive dark-haired girl in her early twenties and

Elizabeth guessed she was the more pleasant of the two housemaids.

"When are you going to sound that gong?" asked Annie.

"We haven't mixed the milk yet," replied Olive.

"Well get a move on. I want to start making up the plates. It must be after seven."

"Only two minutes." Olive glanced in Elizabeth's direction and smirked as if to tell her that the cook's asperity did not bother her. She was a tall, rather thin woman, a few years older than Louise. Her light brown hair was drawn back in a severe style, accentuating her sharp features. She gave a short laugh as a loud clanging noise came from outside the building.

"There's the triangle. I hope you're ready."

"I'm always ready on time. It's you people who're so slow."

Elizabeth felt conspicuous sitting idly while everybody else was occupied, and despite her efforts to remain calm she felt colour mounting into her face again.

Her discomfort was eased by another arrival at the back door. Louise was waiting at the serving table for Annie to produce a batch of completed dinners, and she looked over her shoulder with a smile. "Hi, Charles."

"Hello, Louise."

"Meet our new school teacher — Elizabeth. This is Charles, a kind of general dogsbody."

"How do you do," murmured Elizabeth.

"How do you do." Charles inclined his head, then walked to a chair at the farther end of the table and stood beside it. He was a tall, slim man with fair hair and a lightly tanned complexion. His white shirt was impeccably clean and pressed and his khaki shorts had sharp creases. A faint aroma of talcum powder hung about him and Elizabeth thought how different he was from the image she had built up of bush people. She had never expected to meet a man here who took such care over his appearance.

"Have you started yet?" he asked.

"No, not yet."

"Well, it's not much use waiting for the others. George is always late in on bus days, and Noreen won't come till he's ready. I'll get some soup for you."

He dodged around Annie, poured the soup and carried the plates back to the table.

"You'll soon find out where everything is," he told her. "When you're ready to eat, just start right in. The rest of us are likely to come in and out at any time."

Elizabeth felt more comfortable with company at the table and she enjoyed her dinner. As Mr. Hampton had said, Annie was a good cook. The food had none of the institutional dullness of some hotels, and was tastefully arrayed on the plates. As Charles took her empty plate away, George returned with another woman. She was almost as tall as he, decidedly well-built, with dark brown hair cropped close to her head. She wore a yellow T-shirt and navy blue slacks and looked totally relaxed.

"This is my wife, Noreen," said George.

"Hello," said Noreen. "Have a good trip?"

"Yes, thank you."

"Sorry I wasn't around when you turned up. We've had a cow of a day. Flaming pump broke down, then the generator. I've been messing around trying to get the laundry done for hours. Washing by hand in cold water isn't my idea of fun."

"It must have been very difficult."

"Well, worse things happen. We grouch but we get by."

Noreen served soup for her husband and herself and dropped into the chair beside Elizabeth. She broke a piece of bread into small pieces and tossed them into the soup, then stirred them in with a spoon. As Elizabeth turned to see how Charles obtained the desserts a swift movement caught her eye. She started visibly and could not resist a gasp of dismay as she looked properly at the place where it had happened. A pale beige coloured creature had darted across the corner above the refrigerator and was now running diagonally up the wall.

Noreen slapped the table with her free hand and guffawed loudly. "It's only a gecko," she chortled. "They don't harm anybody. You'll probably see them in your room. They come out after dark."

"In my room?" faltered Elizabeth, watching the

44

creature turn and dart in the opposite direction.

"They're good to have," said George. "They catch flies. Don't worry about them. They won't bother you."

"What next?" sniffed Annie, purporting to talk to herself but audibly enough to be heard by all. "Scared of a mere gecko. That's what comes of taking foreigners in. They should stick to Australians for a place like this."

George began to discuss the generator's problems with Charles to drown her voice and Elizabeth tried to concentrate on her dessert to hide her discomfort. Every so often she glanced back at the wall to see what the gecko was doing. When it disappeared from view she worried about where it had gone, and the arrival of two more on the opposite wall made her quail. Everybody else seemed to accept them as part of the scenery but she could not imagine herself sharing her bedroom with one. Besides, what other creatures could she expect to come creeping out of the woodwork in the night? She should have paid more attention to Jean's warnings.

CHAPTER FIVE

CONTRARY TO all her expectations, Elizabeth slept soundly that night. She had escaped to her cabin immediately after dinner and pottered about arranging her bits and pieces. Soon after nine o'clock she climbed into bed, taking a last look around for any unwelcome creatures before switching off the light. The long journey through the heat that day and the shorter rest than usual the night before ensured that she did not lie awake for long. At first light the raucous cries of crows disturbed her, but the noise faded away and she slipped back into sleep.

It was broad daylight when she awoke again and the sun was high in the sky. The only sounds to be heard were chirps and whistles from birds in nearby trees and bushes. Elizabeth looked at her watch, then sat up abruptly and looked again. Just after half-past nine. How could she have slept so long? Breakfast was at eight o'clock. What a way to start her first day.

By the time she emerged from her cabin it was after ten o'clock. She stood on the doorstep and looked around, wafting flies away from her face. The day was already hot and nobody was in sight. The other cabin doors and windows were firmly closed against the heat, and the only signs of activity were two sprinklers busily spraying water on the lawns. Elizabeth did not relish the prospect of facing Annie and her pointed remarks, but the kitchen seemed the most likely place to find people and learn the Saturday routine so she headed in that direction.

"Hi," came a cheerful voice, as she neared the top of the path.

Elizabeth turned and saw Louise at the window of the cabin she had just passed. "Oh, hello," she said.

"Just up?"

"Yes, I'm afraid so. I don't know how I could have slept so long."

"Easy. Some of this mob stay in bed till lunch-time on their day off. Come in if you like. I've just got to finish off here, then I'll walk over with you. It's just about time for smoke-oh."

Elizabeth went inside and saw Louise running a mop over the bathroom floor.

"Sit down. I won't be a minute. Mark said you'd probably sleep late this morning and left instructions that you were not to be disturbed."

"I see. Where are all the tourists?"

"Some of them are riding. George has taken the rest of them out in the bus." Louise chuckled. "He brings back those who can't make the return horse trip, too."

All the staff except George assembled in the kitchen for tea and hot scones. Despite her sour exterior, Annie had a soft heart and believed in feeding people well.

"Bacon and egg, or chops?" she asked Elizabeth.

"Neither, thank you. I don't eat a large breakfast. Scones will be ideal."

"It won't take a minute."

"No, thank you. I don't eat much at breakfast. Really."

"Well, please yourself. But that's not the way to get strong."

Elizabeth blushed at the reference to the state of her health and Noreen spoke quickly to change the subject.

"What are you going to do with yourself today?"

"I haven't decided yet."

"Why don't you go down to the stables? You'll meet Steve, and it's somewhere to aim for."

The others soon dispersed to their various jobs and Elizabeth decided to take up the suggestion.

"You take a hat," warned Annie as she opened the back door. "We don't want you down with sunstroke — we've got enough to do as it is. You're too fair for these parts."

"I'll take care," answered Elizabeth softly. "Thank you."

The red puppy was sprawled disconsolately outside. His ears pricked as Elizabeth approached and his tail wagged hopefully.

"Hello," said Elizabeth. "Have you been left all on your own? What's your name?"

The puppy sprang up and loped towards her, his body wriggling with delight at the unexpected attention. Elizabeth stooped to pat him and he rolled over and over, rubbing himself against her ankles every time he regained his feet.

"I suppose the difficulty now will be getting rid of you," said Elizabeth. "I wonder if anybody would mind if I took you for a walk?"

She stood upright again and hesitated, then the pleading expression in the puppy's eyes decided her. She returned to the kitchen door and peeped inside.

"Annie, do you think it would be all right if I took the puppy with me?"

"Do what you like with him, as long as you don't let him in here. Dogs! There are too many of them around this place."

As she strolled along the path that had been pointed out to her, Elizabeth felt the same contentment that had enveloped her when she first sat alone in her room. The view of the mountain range, now a different colour in the strong light of day, was magnificent. Perfect peace surrounded her and she thought that here she could regain all her former strength and vitality. Most of the staff seemed friendly towards her, especially Louise, and she would soon get used to the others. Even Annie seemed concerned about her welfare, under that brusque attitude. Elizabeth smiled fondly at the puppy as it bounded back from investigating a clump of grass. He at least was definitely glad of her company.

A short stocky man wearing dusty jeans and high-heeled riding boots came out of the shed as Elizabeth drew close to the yard. He ambled towards the gate and waited there for her.

"You'll be Miss Gaunt, the new teacher, I reckon."

"That's right. But please call me Elizabeth. Everybody else does."

"Okay — Elizabeth. I'm Steve. I can't offer to shake hands. I've been doing some messy work."

"That's all right. People don't seem to do that sort of thing very much, anyway."

"No, I reckon not."

He gazed at her pale, clear complexion and her slender arms, showing a trace of pink from exposure to the sun yesterday. He wished that floppy hat didn't hide so much of her hair. He'd heard what an attractive silver colour it was. "You'd better come under the trees. Don't want to get too much sun all at once."

"Is it all right if the puppy comes in?"

"Sure. Aren't any horses in at present anyway, but he'll need to get used to them." He jerked his thumb in the direction of the shed, where a sturdy dog stood in the doorway. "I left him there in case you were scared of dogs. Want to meet him?"

"Oh, yes please."

"Okay, Bluey, come on."

The dog leapt forward and sniffed briefly at

Elizabeth's feet, then turned his attention to the puppy. It cringed immediately, but gradually gained confidence and became playful.

"That's an unusual dog," exclaimed Elizabeth as it gambolled away with the puppy. "I've never seen one like it before."

"He's a blue heeler," came the proud reply. "Best dogs you can get. Cost me a packet but I wouldn't change him. D'you mind if I smoke?"

"No, of course not." Elizabeth watched as Steve opened one of the many pouches on his broad leather belt. He pulled out a packet of cigarette papers and some loose tobacco and deftly rolled a cigarette by hand.

"You're not dressed for riding, so I don't suppose you wanted a horse this morning," he said.

"No, I can't ride."

"Easy enough, especially on these old stock horses. Soon as you've got settled in, come on down and try it." He made an unsuccessful attempt to blow smoke rings and looked at her with interest. "What in the world made you come to a place like this, anyway?"

Elizabeth shrugged as casually as possible. "Well, I wanted somewhere quiet and this sounded so attractive." To divert the conversation from herself she asked him a question. "Do you live up there with the others? I didn't see you at dinner."

"No, I live down there." He pointed out a track winding on past the yard rails, and she saw the sun glinting on a galvanised iron roof beyond a clump of desert oaks. "The wife's in town at present. She had a baby a few days ago. Our first."

"Oh." Elizabeth swallowed hard, then continued calmly,"How nice. It must be exciting for you."

"Yeah. A seven and a quarter pound girl. Very pretty, so I've heard."

"Your wife must be sorry you're not with her."

"Well, that's how it goes out here. I flew in, but it turned out to be a false alarm. After that we decided to let things be. I'll be seeing them soon enough now."

They both sat on an old log at the foot of a mulga tree, Steve enlarging on his news about the baby. He was fond of his wife, no doubt about that, and Elizabeth relaxed. His obvious interest in her and his ready offer to teach her how to ride were nothing more than interest in a stranger and his normal friendly manner. He would have acted the same way with anybody. She felt more comfortable with him than anybody she had met in months, and when the conversation returned to her journey and arrival she answered quite naturally.

Soon Steve discovered her timidity about insects and other wildlife.

"I felt quite brave in Adelaide," she admitted. "I was telling everybody how well I would cope with all the things they mentioned, but now I'm not so sure." She sighed. "Even the lizards scare me. Geckoes, I mean."

Unlike the others, Steve did not laugh. "It's the quick way they move that frightens you," he said seriously. "If you keep watch on them when they're still you'll find they're quite beautiful."

He smiled at her doubtful face. "There's nothing much to worry about up here," he told her. "There are plenty of red back spiders, but all you have to do about them is take care. Always look underneath things before you handle them, like under tables. Red backs prefer dark places." He glanced down at her open-toed sandals. "Got any proper shoes with you?"

"Yes, I was told to bring rubber soled shoes."

"Wear them at night outside, then you won't run into trouble with centipedes or scorpions." He laughed and lifted his feet off the ground to emphasise his words. "You won't find me out without my boots, especially after dark. Some of the others go around in bare feet or thongs all the time."

He opened the pouch on his belt to roll another cigarette and Elizabeth gasped aloud. Only a few inches away from her knee a piece of dirty straw had started to move. She looked again and saw to her horror that it had sprouted legs.

"That's a stick insect," chuckled Steve. He stretched his arm across her and gently picked it up. "Perfect disguise, isn't it? You have to be careful not to snap their legs because they're very fragile, but you can make pets out of these. Kids love them."

"I suppose I'll have to be prepared for the children

bringing these kind of things inside," sighed Elizabeth.

"Don't let them see you're nervous or they'll give you a terrible time. Carl, anyway. He's a real prankster."

He talked about the insect's habits, speaking with such knowledge and obvious love of nature that Elizabeth's interest began to grow. She even gained enough confidence to allow the stick insect to walk across her hand, and was amazed at the delicate high steps it made, not tickling her in the slightest.

By the time the tourists were due to return with the horses she and Steve were firm friends and had arranged to walk over to the sandhills the following afternoon to look at wild flowers.

"It's been good talking to you," said Steve, helping her to her feet. "I'll take you down to the bore at sunset tomorrow and you might see one or two animals."

He gave a short whistle and Bluey scrambled out from beneath a tractor. The puppy followed, making a great fuss of Elizabeth when he reached her again.

"You rogue, you had forgotten you were supposed to be with me," she laughed. "Good-bye, Steve. Thank you very much for everything."

The sun felt stronger than before when she left the shelter of the tree and the walk back was harder. On the way to the stables she had not noticed the incline, but now it seemed steeper than it really was. Elizabeth reached the buildings at last, her eyes dazzled by light striking up from the red earth, her throat and mouth parched.

"You look as though you need a drink," called Noreen. "Come in through the dining-room and save yourself the walk round the back."

Elizabeth stepped into the room where Olive was laying cutlery on one of the large circular tables. Noreen was behind the bar, leaning casually on the counter and regarding Elizabeth with amusement.

"Hot enough for you?"

"It certainly is," answered Elizabeth, taking off her hat and fanning herself with it. "I suppose I should save my walking for early morning or late afternoon."

"You'll get used to it. Have a beer."

"No, not beer," replied Elizabeth sharply. Drink was one thing she would never touch, that was certain. Drink had been the cause of that horror. If Jack hadn't been drinking that night and started that party on the deck... Elizabeth dashed the memory away and looked up at Noreen again. The amusement had gone and she was staring at her with concern.

"I'm sorry," said Elizabeth shakily. "I didn't mean to be rude. It's just — it's just that I don't drink beer and things."

"I'll get you a lemonade. Sit down, you look dreadful. That sun must have really got at you."

It was easier to let everybody think she had become over-heated, rather than attempt to explain.

It was useless trying to explain, anyway, thought Elizabeth listlessly. Nobody could imagine the effects of haunting memories unless they had suffered badly themselves. She sat on the chair that Olive pushed towards her and let them fuss without restraint. Soon she felt calm again, and seeing the colour return to her cheeks the two women decided that their administrations had cured her.

George came back with his tourists, bringing a cheerful air to the kitchen. Elizabeth felt far more at ease than she had the evening before and even found an appetite for the salad lunch.

"Where does Mrs. Hampton get to all day?" she asked, during a lull in conversation. "She must be the only person I haven't met."

An awkward silence followed her words. Olive stopped abruptly on her way to the dining-room with a tray of desserts, and everybody turned to stare at Elizabeth.

"There isn't any Mrs. Hampton," said Noreen at last. "She died about five years ago, soon after Pauline was born."

"So they say," put in Annie, gathering her utensils together with unnecessary clatter. "Always strikes me as strange that nobody ever mentions her. Not even Margaret, and she must be old enough to remember her."

"Oh dear," whispered Elizabeth.

"You don't mean to say he never told you?" demanded Olive.

Elizabeth floundered in confusion. It would never do to let them know what a shock the news had been to her, especially that interfering cook.

"Well, no, he couldn't have."

"And how do you account for that?" asked Annie.

"Well, I suppose the subject just didn't come up," answered Elizabeth weakly.

Annie grumbled on about haphazard arrangements and lack of efficiency and Elizabeth stared down at her teacup. Would she have come if he had told her he had no wife, no mother for his children? Useless to ponder over that now, it was too late. Elizabeth sighed deeply. She had thought she was coming to a well-knit family with no problems or threat of involvement for herself, but instead she had walked right into the kind of situation she had been trying to avoid. Even Mr. Hampton's special efforts to make her comfortable became suspect in the light of this new information. It was quite possible that he had encouraged her to come up here for all the wrong reasons.

CHAPTER SIX

ELIZABETH LEFT the kitchen as soon as she thought she could do so without seeming to be impolite. As she closed the door it occurred to her that she had not seen or heard any of the children since they had hurried off to dinner the previous evening, but she would have expected five youngsters to make their presence felt. As if aware that they had been missed, the children had gathered around the corner, waiting or her to appear.

"Hello," said Elizabeth. "I was wondering where you had all got to."

"We went to the sandhills for a picnic," said Carl.

"My goodness, it must have been hot."

"Yes, that's why we're not allowed to stay away longer than two hours by ourselves."

"We know a nice shady spot," added Pauline.

"Good. You'll have to show me sometime."

They nodded, the only two of the group who did not look ill at ease. Julie was half hidden behind Margaret and Brian edged away slightly when Elizabeth smiled at him. He nudged Margaret and she took a small step forward.

"Dad said I've got to show you how the radio

works, ready for school on Monday."

"I hope it's not hard."

"No. You won't have to use it anyway. We do it ourselves."

"Good. Is everybody coming?"

"If they want," replied Margaret grudgingly.

"You'll see our new schoolroom, too," said Pauline, clinging to Elizabeth's hand and dancing along as if the heat had no effect.

"How nice. Are you looking forward to starting on Monday?"

"Rather. I'm lucky, aren't I, having a proper school and a proper teacher? The others didn't when they first started."

There was no need for Elizabeth to reply for the little girl immediately chattered on about her new coloured pencils that someone had given her for Christmas. Elizabeth noticed the scornul expression on Margaret's face and smiled understandingly at her. Her eldest pupil obviously had no love for schoolwork.

They crossed a stretch of ground behind the tourists' accommodation, heading towards a low, modern bungalow surrounded by a lawn and a row of colourful croton bushes.

"This is our house," said Carl as they mounted the veranda steps. "We're using a different room for lessons this year, so that we can get a table in for Pauline."

The room was at the back of the house with a

splendid view of the sandhills. Elizabeth took a brief glimpse out of the window, then turned her attention to the furnishings. Three tables stood in a row, each a different height, with five chairs neatly spaced behind them, all facing the same direction.

"Steve made that," said Pauline, pointing.

Elizabeth looked around and saw a large blackboard fastened to the wall opposite the chairs. She touched it gingerly and found it was perectly smooth.

"He used proper blackboard stuff to paint it with," said Brian.

"It's very good," answered Elizabeth. "I hope we've got plenty of chalk."

"There's a whole boxful."

Elizabeth was relieved that Brian had spoken to her at last. He had seemed much too withdrawn for a boy of his age, hiding behind Margaret's personality. Only Julie needed to come out of her shell now. She still avoided Elizabeth's gaze and had a tendency to suck her thumb.

"The radio's over here," said Margaret, determined to get her task over with as soon as possible.

She led Elizabeth to the corner and gestured towards a low wooden cabinet where the radio stood. It was smaller than Elizabeth had expected, without complicated dials that she had feared. A pad of plain paper lay beside it and a ball point pen attached to a piece of string. Margaret picked up the microphone and tilted it to show a shiny button to Elizabeth.

"You've got to keep that pressed down all the time you're talking. You let it go when you've stopped talking."

"I see."

"You turn the radio on here." Margaret flicked a switch and crackling noises illed the room. "If reception's bad you can try the other wave length, but we're supposed to stay on this one. That's our call sign." She pointed to a bell pasted on the front of the casing and switched off. "That's all. Easy, isn't it?"

"Yes, it seems to be," answered Elizabeth. The demonstration had apparently ended.

"Do you need us for anything else?"

"Not just now, thank you. Have you got your lessons from last year?" The girl nodded and Elizabeth went on, "Bring them in here on Monday morning please, so that I can see what you have been doing recently. And everybody bring your favourite book."

"A book?" echoed Carl.

"Yes, please. Your own, not a school one."

"Okay." Margaret shrugged and turned to leave, but before she reached the door her father tapped and entered.

"May I come in?"

"Of course," answered Elizabeth.

"Is everything satisfactory in here?"

"Yes, thank you." Elizabeth glanced again at the

row of tables and the bare walls. She could soon make this room look more friendly and interesting. "There's much more space than I was expecting."

"This room will probably serve a more useful purpose now than it has in the past. Have the children shown you everything you want to know?"

"Yes, thank you."

"If there's anything you want, tell me. They've all got pencils and rubbers and things, but if there's anything else needed you only have to ask." He looked at the children, hovering near the door so that they could leave at the first opportunity. "You mind what I told you about working hard this term. You've all got to improve a lot." They nodded and he clicked his fingers. "All right, if Miss Gaunt doesn't want you any longer you can go."

He grinned as the children scampered away. "Can't get out of here quick enough. I hope they don't give you any bother next week."

"I'm quite sure they won't, Mr. Hampton."

"Call me Mark. I don't go for this Mister business. You must have noticed that everybody else calls me Mark."

"I had, yes, but somehow it doesn't seem right to..."

"You can't be stand-offish in a place like this. I want you to feel at home, like one of the family."

"But..."

"You'll get used to it soon enough," he interrupted. "I know this kind of life is different to

62

anything you've experienced before, but I hope you'll be happy here."

Elizabeth looked away from his earnest ace. He was apparently only too willing to disregard the gulf that usually lay between employer and employee, but she never wanted to feel close to anyone again. If he pressed his attentions upon her she would have to leave, no matter what dierence it made to the children's future. Mark sensed her withdrawal and laughed lightly.

"I know we must seem an uncouth mob to you at times, but we can't afford to stand on ceremony in a place like this. Everybody piles in to help when need be, whatever their real job is."

"I don't want to seem snobbish for anything. It's not that I disapprove of the way of life here, but it just isn't natural for me to be like that."

Had it been one of the other girls, Mark would have flung an arm around her shoulders and jollied her out of her seriousness. But this one was too refined for such treatment and her manner was beginning to make him feel inept. He had better stick to business and hope she lost some of that icy shell when she had settled in properly.

"I expect you'd like to look through the first week's papers from the Correspondence School," he said.

"Yes, please. It will help me to prepare the lessons."

They were both relieved by the return to a formal

footing. Mark hastened to an adjoining room and returned with five bulky envelopes.

"Anytime you want to work in here, walk straight in," he told her. "You don't want to be carting stuff to and fro." He waved one hand impatiently as she opened her lips to speak. "Treat this like an ordinary schoolroom, and remember you're in charge. You don't need to worry about disturbing me. I'm hardly around anyway, except early afternoon. We usually give the tourists time to rest after lunch, especially in the summer, but I find something to do in the main building more often than not."

"I see."

Mark handed the envelopes to her, and as there seemed nothing else to be done she moved towards the door.

"How about joining the tourists tomorrow?" he asked her suddenly. "You'll be organised by then. We're taking a trip to the ranges." "No thank you, not this weekend."

"Why not? You can't possibly expect to spend your time working. The lessons are already set out for you in there." His voice softened as he tried to coax her. "You'll enjoy the sunset on the ranges. People come hundreds of miles to see that."

"As a matter of fact, Steve promised to show me around tomorrow. I'm hoping to see some animals at sunset."

"Oh. Well, I'm glad you won't be shut away in your cabin instead of enjoying yourself. Steve will look after you all right." He escorted her to the veranda. "Perhaps next weekend then?" he suggested.

Elizabeth smiled back at him. If she were to live here she would have to make an effort to be sociable. "Next weekend would be very nice. Thank you."

She fully intended to study the school papers that afternoon, but she could not concentrate. Either the climate for the emotional strain, or a mixture of both, had tired her. For several minutes she fought against sleepiness, sitting upright on the straight chair in her room, but eventually she gave in and lay on the bed. There was the entire evening to come and another full day tomorrow before starting to teach. Plenty of time yet.

She slept for an hour, after which she felt remarkably fresh. She washed her face and combed her hair into place, then settled down to read the lessons for next week. It seemed to her that if the governesses had been as poor as their reputations and the children had done no more than the actual contents of the lessons, they would be far below the standard she had come to expect from her pupils. Glittering results could not be hoped for too soon.

"Elizabeth, are you awake?" came a soft voice from outside.

She looked up quickly. "Oh, Noreen! Yes, I am. Come in."

Noreen entered with her usual lack of ceremony. She was wearing yellow shorts this afternoon, which fitted closely and emphasised the thickness of her bulky thighs. Above them she wore a black sun top, exposing a wide expanse of tanned flesh.

"Wow!" she exclaimed, glancing at the array of booklets around Elizabeth before flopping into the easy chair. "No sleep this afternoon?"

"I did sleep for a while. I just couldn't keep my eyes open. But I've got through a bit of work since then."

Noreen watched her gathering the lessons together. "How d'you think the kids'll make out?"

"Once we get used to each other they'll be all right. At least I hope so." Elizabeth gazed at the other woman thoughtfully. "I can't understand why the children seem so nervous. They don't seem natural somehow."

Noreen gave a short laugh. "That'll be some of Annie's doing, I expect. She's always saying they need proper discipline and they probably think you're here to give it. Mark's been laying it on a bit thick, too, telling them they'll have to behave now they've got a proper teacher."

"No wonder they were scared of me. People shouldn't put children off school like that."

"Well, Mark's getting a bit desperate. The last governess got the sack for being drunk and nobody did much about supervising towards the end of last term. I rather gather that the school sent a disapproving letter."

Don't worry. They'll soon find out that you're not

66

an old bear. You got a shock at lunch-time, didn't you?" she asked unexpectedly.

"A shock? Oh, you mean when I asked about Mrs. Hampton's wife." Elizabeth blushed again as she remembered that terrible moment. "That was an awful thing to happen. I couldn't have been more embarrassed. Just imagine, I might have said something when he was there."

"Serve him right for not telling you," returned Noreen unfeelingly.

"He never mentioned a wie, but I assumed he had one. I suppose I ought to know by now, not to take anything for granted."

There was a short silence as they recalled the scene in the kitchen. Noreen was still amused at the other's *faux pas,* but Elizabeth was puzzling over Annie's cryptic remarks. She felt guilty about gossiping over her employer's affairs, but if she were to understand the family she ought to know something about their background.

"What was Annie getting at?" she asked at last. "When she said something about people only *saying* that Mrs. Hampton was dead?"

Noreen licked her hand scornully. "Take no notice. That's only Annie again. I've heard it said in town there's something funny about her going, but that's only because they don't know the true story. I suppose they think they might find out if they try to start a scandal." She leaned forward, more seriously than Elizabeth had yet seen her. "She did die. That much I'm sure of. Some folk reckon she only left him and he never mentions her because he's still sulking, but that's all hogwash. Mrs. Chapman knows all about it. She's our regular cook and she was here when it happened. She never says much either. Mark seems to blame himself for what happened, so it must have been some kind of accident."

"It's hard for the children, never hearing anything about their mother."

"Yeah, I suppose so, but they must be used to it by now." Noreen leaned back in her chair and grinned mischievously again. "Anyway, maybe Olive'll be sweeter to you now. It was obvious to everyone that you didn't know Mark was a widower."

Elizabeth was confused. "What difference does that make?"

"Well, it means you didn't come up here as a competitor."

"You mean..."

"Yeah, she's got her hooks in him. Why else do you think she's stayed so long up here? It must have been a slap in the eye for her when you turned up, all smart and attractive."

Elizabeth flushed. "Well, she needn't worry. I certainly have no designs on him — for anybody else come to that."

"Don't be too sure about that," teased Noreen. "Mark's not a bad bloke, you know, and you might easily fall for him if he gets into a marrying frame of mind again."

"I shall do nothing of the sort," declared Elizabeth hotly. "I have no intention of marrying anybody."

"You say that now, but wait till you meet the right one. Love's a funny thing that just happens. Right out of the blue. Wham." Noreen clapped her hands together. "It hasn't happened to you yet, but it will one day."

Elizabeth managed to bite back the hasty retort that flew to her lips, but Noreen saw the stricken look on her ace. "Oh dear. Have I said something I shouldn't?"

Elizabeth took a deep breath. "It's all right. I was the one who almost said something I shouldn't."

"I've upset you," said Noreen contritely. "I'm sorry. Me and my big mouth."

"It's quite all right."

"Let's go and get a cup of tea then." Noreen pulled herself to her feet, anxious to end the embarrassing episode. "We usually make a pot at four to put Annie in a good, mood for starting the dinner."

CHAPTER SEVEN

AFTER LUNCH the next day Louise showed Elizabeth the lounge and she stared in delight at the array of books along one wall.

"Enough there to keep you occupied for quite a while," laughed Louise.

"There certainly are. Do you read much, Louise?"

"Not really. Some of the tourists leave paperbacks behind — love stories and that — but there isn't much in my line up there."

"I'll come back later and investigate," said Elizabeth. She loved books and her pleasure would be spoiled if someone were standing by waiting, no matter how patient they managed to be.

"Stay and look at them now if you like. I'll have to be off and get some washing done."

There were five long rows of books, some volumes hardly touched, others tatty and fingermarked. They were pushed

anyhow into a place, biographies, crime stories, travel, novels and westerns all mixed up in total confusion. One day she must sort them all out, thought Elizabeth. She did not hear the door opening and the sudden low voice made her jump "I see you're interested in the books."

"Oh." Elizabeth whirled around, clutching two books closely to her body.

"I'm sorry I startled you," said Mark. He thrust his hands into his pockets and watched her face anxiously. "I didn't mean to give you a shock."

"It's all right," answered Elizabeth. She relaxed and smiled at him to prove she was feeling quite calm again. "I must have been too engrossed. I didn't hear a sound until you spoke."

"I'll bang the door next time. You can borrow any books you like. I suppose you realise that."

Elizabeth glanced back at the crammed shelves and the pile of extra books lying on a side table. There was no chance of anybody keeping track of them.

"Don't you lose a lot?" she asked. "No one would ever know what the tourists had borrowed, and some people have a bad habit of keeping books."

Mark shrugged. "Doesn't make much dierence. Nobody else here is interested much. It's usually the long staying guests who do the most reading and they manage to finish what they've started." He grinned. "Anyway, people seem to be pretty honest. They must forget their city ways when they get out here. We've had books sent back through the post a few times when people couldn't finish in time and took them away."

"There's a wonderul selection here."

"Yes, I suppose so." Mark regarded the shelves

thoughtfully. "The tourists appreciate them, so they're doing far more good here than cluttering up my place — even if a few of them do disappear. Anyway, they'd never be opened otherwise. If the whole lot went at least I'd know they'd gone where they would be used."

"Do you mean to say that you don't read much yourself?" exclaimed Elizabeth. "Not with a collection like this?"

"No, they weren't mine." He hesitated, as i he might explain further, but changed his mind. He turned away from the bookshelves and stared out of the window. They must have belonged to his wife, thought Elizabeth. That mysterious wife who had died so long ago, whom he had not yet mentioned. He could not bring himself to speak of her. He must have loved her very much.

"I'll have to check the tucker box," he said, swinging around suddenly. "Help yourself to anything you like. You can wander anywhere, you know, and mix with the tourists if you feel like a bit of company."

He strode out of the room, intent on preparations for the trip that afternoon. Elizabeth watched him go, suspecting that he concentrated on business matters whenever he needed distraction from painful memories. She sighed heavily. She had come here in an effort to conquer the effects of the past. It seemed that she and her employer had a problem in common.

The slight lapse into depression ended as soon as

she opened another book. She decided to take that one with her and returned to her cabin, reading contentedly until it was time to meet Steve. As she made her way across the grass to the path the red puppy gambolled over to her.

"Anyone would think you knew I would be setting off for a walk right now," she laughed, bending down to pat him. "I suppose you might as well come along. Nobody yearns to be with you."

The puppy trotted along beside her as if it had never doubted that an invitation would be orthcoming. Steve grinned as he watched them approach the stables together, and Bluey scrambled up, his tail wagging a greeting.

"That pup seems to have attached itself to you."

"I don't know where he suddenly appeared rom. I hadn't seen him until I set o to come down here."

"They can sense walks from two miles away," laughed Steve. "He'll be glad you came. Nobody else bothers with him much, but he'll grow into a good dog given the chance."

"I'm surprised the children don't pay more attention to him."

"They play with him when they're around the buildings," answered Steve, rubbing his boot gently against the wriggling body. "But they've got their own special pet and they're very loyal to her. This one was brought down from the station. A bit of a mistake, they were hoping for pure breds, but he's got some good blood in him by the looks of things."

"Has he got a name yet?"

Steve chuckled." Annie Fenn has special names for all of them. She's not very fond of dogs. This one was called Rufus, though, because of his red coat." He pinched out the stub of his cigarette and ground it carefully into the dirt with his boot. "I've just got one more last job to do," he told her, lifting a heavy sack and slinging it onto his shoulder. "Won't take a minute. By the time you've looked at the horses I'll be through."

Elizabeth returned full of enthusiasm about her first sight of wild kangaroos, and ready to give an account of her jaunt. Steve had accepted an invitation to dinner and everybody except Olive, who had gone with the coach, gathered around the table to eat together. Even Annie was more sociable than usual, her normally acid remarks toned down, and Elizabeth was told that Sunday was often the easiest day of the week. All the tourists went to the ranges for a barbecue dinner, leaving them in peace until almost ten o'clock.

They shared the clearing away and washing up, then gathered in the games room. Noreen, Steve, Annie and Louise played a oursome at table tennis, while Charles invited Elizabeth to learn pool, which she discovered was similar to snooker. He was immaculately dressed in carefully ironed shirt and shorts as before, and treated Elizabeth with an old-world courtesy that made her eel like an important person. He seemed to be a model of patience, placing balls where they should be easy to hit, and consoling her when she missed.

Monday morning was a complete contrast to that easy-going atmosphere. Olive and Louise were dashing about, trying to serve breakast in less time than usual because all the tourists were leaving on the coach and the earlier they started the better. Annie was back to her normal state, commenting furiously on the idiosyncracies of guests who all demanded their eggs cooked a different way, and Noreen was packing the tucker box with lunch that had to be eaten in the open air along the route. George was busy checking the coach and Charles had apparently finished breakast an hour ago and started work.

Elizabeth helped herself to toast and tea, feeling awkward and in the way. As soon as she had eaten she hurried outside and walked across to the bungalow. She would feel more at home in the schoolroom, even if it were different from any she had worked in before.

The children were playing in an adjoining room. Elizabeth could hear Carl and Pauline talking as she wrote the date on the blackboard. True to character they were chattering loudly and naturally, but the others only answered with whispers for an occasional subdued giggle. At five minutes to nine they all filed in with books tucked beneath their arms and stood in a row before her.

"Good morning, everybody," said Elizabeth

brightly.

"Good morning, Miss Gaunt," they chorused.

They were all wearing shoes and socks this morning and their hair was tidily brushed. Elizabeth smiled as she remembered the state they were in on Saturday afternoon, barefooted, their hair and clothes thick with red dust.

"You're all looking very smart this morning," she said. "I want a photograph of you on the first day of term, so I think I had better take it now before you get messed up."

"What do you want a photograph of us or?" asked Carl.

"To keep as a reminder of the first day. And I want to send one to my brother and his wife in Adelaide. They'll be interested to see what you all look like."

"Are you taking it in colour?" asked Brian.

"Yes. You need coloured photographs to show how beautiul it is here."

None of them seemed enthusiastic, but they left their belongings on a table as she instructed and followed her outside. Elizabeth fought down a sigh as she watched them gathering into a group. How strange these children were. All the others she had known would have rushed to have their photographs taken.

Her next surprise came when the children presented the books that were supposed to be their favourites. Margaret had a weekly magazine, Carl and Brian had annuals that were mainly composed of pictures and Julie had an old fairy tale book with Margaret's name in it. Pauline came to the table last with a painting book almost filled with childish scribbles.

"A magazine isn't really what I was expecting, Margaret," she said, trying not to sound critical. "Haven't you got a proper book that you like?"

"They're all too young," answered Margaret. "They're soft."

"Oh dear. Haven't people chosen the right kind for you?"

"I haven't had any since I was about eight."

"Haven't you? But your…" Elizabeth cut herself short. Thinking of the display of books in the lounge she had almost mentioned the children's mother and that was apparently taboo in this household. "When did any of you last get a new book?" she asked.

The children looked at each other uncertainly.

"We all got painting books for Christmas," said Pauline helpfully.

"Those annuals came last," said Margaret. "One of the housemaids gave them to Carl and Brian the Christmas before."

Elizabeth managed to hide her dismay. "If you haven't read many books you have a lot to look forward to," she said. "Now, how about rearranging this classroom? We don't want everybody sitting in a row."

The children had assumed that they would be

made to sit down and begin hard work as soon as the clock on the mantelpiece showed nine o'clock. Her informal attitude was a relief, and as they pushed the tables and chairs into different positions they began to feel better. Perhaps a real teacher was not so fierce after all. Elizabeth found them little jobs to do, making them feel useful and talking to them all the time in a friendly way to gain their confidence.

School of the Air was due to start at nine forty-five, and when the school music began even Margaret looked interested. Pauline was quivering with excitement at being able to take part in the lessons for the first time, and as soon as roll call was announced Carl snatched up the microphone and shouted the call sign for Desert Oak Ranch. All the children spoke to the teacher while Elizabeth sat thankfully silent. As Margaret had said, there was no need for her to be nervous of the radio lessons. The children could handle the set easily by themselves.

The rest of the morning passed much as Elizabeth had expected. Pauline tackled everything with zest, but it was obvious that earlier lessons would have to be repeated for the others.

Lunch-time found the kitchen calm and easy-going. The hectic rush o the morning was forgotten and everybody assembled at the table in good humour. Even Mark strolled in and took a seat opposite Elizabeth.

"How's it going with the kids?" he asked.

"Very well, thank you." Elizabeth hesitated then

continued, "Mr. Hampton, I'd like to talk to you sometime when you have a spare minute.'

"Huh! Mr. Hampton!" scoffed Noreen. "Good lord, don't call him that. You'll have him big-headed and telling everybody to call him that if you're not careful."

"I told you to call me Mark," he chided.

Elizabeth blushed. She wished she could control that rush o blood to her ace, but the fact that she failed usually helped to make her embarrassment worse. Mark watched in amusement, managing to keep a bland expression. The other female members of the staff were fairly hard-boiled and sometimes even bordered on the coarse side. How refreshing it was to see someone actually blush, especially at a more mature age as she was.

"I'm sorry," said Elizabeth. "I'll try to remember."

"The others'll probably make sure you do." he answered. "I take it you want to talk about the kids. How'll it be if I see you in the schoolroom after you've finished?"

"Thank you. That will do very nicely."

CHAPTER EIGHT

AT THE end of the last lessons the children tidied away quickly and disappeared into the open air. Their voices had scarcely faded from the corner of the house when Mark tapped on the door.

"You having trouble with those kids?" he asked.

"Trouble?" repeated Elizabeth. "Goodness me, no. They're perfectly well behaved."

"That's all right then." Mark relaxed visibly and came into the room, staring at the newly arranged furniture. "I see you've made some changes in here already."

"Yes, we don't need to have everybody facing the same way and it's more cosy like this. It gives us a big space in the middle for doing things on the floor, too."

Mark thought back to his own school days of rigid routine. He could not imagine what kind of activities she would encourage on the floor but thought it better not to ask. "I see. What was it you wanted to talk about?"

"About books, actually."

"Books?"

"The children haven't had any new books for over

80

a year, and Margaret says she hasn't had any since she was eight."

"They never said they wanted any. I didn't think they were interested."

"They haven't been interested, that's the whole point. Their reading is poor, and unless they have some books they like they won't see any purpose in trying to improve."

Mark shrugged his shoulders and smiled broadly. "That's soon settled. Can you get enough for your needs with fifty dollars?"

"Fifty dollars?" gasped Elizabeth.

"Isn't that enough?"

"It's plenty. You don't need to spend as much as that."

Mark shrugged again. "Don't be frightened of spending money. I've got enough. Look, you order all the books that'll come in handy. Spend more than fifty dollars if you like."

"Well, thank you." Elizabeth struggled to maintain her line of thought. "I think I'll write to my sister-in-law and ask her to get them for us. She can pick and choose between the different editions."

"Okay. Tell her to send them to Alice on the train. George'll pick 'em up." Mark thrust his hands into his pockets and grinned again as he watched her expression. She had been expecting questions and perhaps opposition so that she would have to argue her case. His unexpected generosity had taken her completely by surprise.

"Don't worry about expense," he told her. "Anything you want, just order it and I'll pay. If lack of books and equipment is your only problem we're in luck."

Elizabeth frowned at his last words. He always seemed to be hinting that her job would not run smoothly.

"Er — Mark —" The use of his first name still caused her embarrassment.

"Yeah?" His grin widened at her hesitation.

"You seem to have the idea that your children are difficult to handle."

"Hm." Mark's amusement evaporated. He stared sheepishly at the floor, shifting his feet like some of her former pupils. "You haven't found them that way?"

"Not at all. In fact they're so quiet and still they don't seem natural. They act as though they're repressed."

"They must have taken the warning to heart then.' Expecting more, Elizabeth waited for him to go on and at last he continued, "I told you that the governesses hadn't been satisactory, didn't I? The last one deinitely wasn't — she drank too much — but I think it was the kids' fault that the others weren't much good. They couldn't control the kids. They really played up and the girls gave in and let."

"They haven't given me that impression," declared Elizabeth. "They seem quite willing, and I think they'll enjoy their lessons when they find they can do them more easily."

"Let's hope they stay that way. They probably will. I told them a real teacher knows how to use a cane."

"Oh dear."

Mark looked up at her disapproving ace. "You don't believe in caning kids when they misbehave then?"

"They won't need it."

"Well, you have my permission to cane as hard and as often as you like if you do find it necessary. Now then, how about a cup of tea in the kitchen to get over your first day?"

His dog, Bruce, was waiting in the passage. He rose leisurely and wagged a greeting, then quietly followed them outside. Elizabeth marvelled again at the impact of the sun as they crossed the threshold. It was so easy to forget the intense heat outside when working in an air-conditioned building. She was about to comment on it, but the red puppy gambolled across and rubbed himself against her ankles, distracting her attention.

"Rufus has adopted you apparently," said Mark.

"He seems to have. Do you mind?"

"No, why should I? A dog needs a companion and I'm already owned by Bruce."

They strolled across the flat open space, the puppy doing his best to entice the older dog into a game.

"Annie thinks it's disgraceful, keeping the kids

out here," said Mark suddenly.

Elizabeth looked up at his unusually solemn ace, and by mutual agreement they changed direction towards a sprawling acacia tree.

"Annie reckons the kids should be at school," he said as they paused in the patch of shade. "Do you think they're being deprived kept here with no other children to play with? And no mother."

It was the first time he had mentioned the children's mother and the pain was evident in his voice.

"No, I don't think they're deprived," answered Elizabeth slowly. "People are coming and going all the time so they're not really isolated out here. And I'm sure you love them. That's more important than anything."

"Yes, I love them." He sighed and ran his fingers through his hair. "I know I don't give them as much time as I ought to, being so busy with the tourists, but I keep them here because I love them. I only hope I'm doing the best for them, and not just being selfish."

"I think it's best." Elizabeth spoke firmly to give him the assurance he so obviously needed.

"Well, I hope you don't have reason to change your mind later, though I've told the kids you're their last chance. Annie is very outspoken on the subject, as you'll discover soon enough if you haven't done so already. Let me know if she becomes offensive, though, and I'll deal with her.

She takes too much on herself more often than not." Mark sighed heavily. "I keep telling myself I should get rid of her. She upsets the tourists when she comes into contact with them, but I can't be bothered to go through all the effort of trying to find another cook. The girls seem to stand up to her all right in the kitchen and Mrs. Chapman will be back at Easter, thank goodness."

In an effort to find a new subject and turn the conversation to a lighter note, Elizabeth looked at her surroundings.

"Where do the children get to all the time?" she asked. "They disappeared as soon as school was over and I hardly saw them all weekend."

"They'll be out with Bess somewhere. The poor dog's been miserable all day. She used to have Pauline to keep her company, but now even she's in school with the others."

They strolled on again towards the kitchen. Olive was watching their approach from the window and her frown deepened into a scowl as Mark rested his arm lightly across Elizabeth's shoulder to usher her inside.

"A large cup of tea for the teacher, Noreen," he called jovially. "She's just suffered her first day."

"Good lord, was it as bad as that?" laughed Noreen.

"Not really," answered Elizabeth, slipping away from Mark's side. "They're much better behaved than Mark would have us believe."

"Well, congratulations, you've got his name right at last. Here we are." Noreen flourished the huge teapot. "Sit yourself down."

She poured out four cups of tea, then flopped onto a chair beside Elizabeth and rested her right ankle on her left knee. "Did Mark warn you that you'll have to make do with my cooking tonight? Annie's day off. I cook Monday dinner and all meals on Tuesday."

"I expect I'll survive if the others can," answered Elizabeth. It was easy to respond to Noreen's nonchalant ways.

"Yeah. Well Mark never trusts me with the tourists, except for salads and suchlike. If anybody's staying here he always takes them out for a barbecue on Tuesdays."

"There's a plane in tomorrow," said Mark. He seated himself opposite Elizabeth, and as an afterthought pulled out a chair for Olive who had followed him to the table. "If you want any letters posted, Elizabeth, have them ready by lunch-time tomorrow and the pilot will take them to town."

"Thank you. I'll get a list of books ready this evening."

Mark leaned forward and helped himself to sugar, spooning the usual large amount into his cup. "Talking of barbecues, why don't you come with the party tomorrow, Elizabeth?"

Elizabeth looked up and met the clear hostility in Olive's eyes. "Oh, well," she stammered, not failing to understand and the reason for the other woman's enmity. "I don't know…"

"Nonsense. There's plenty of room and we don't leave till four o'clock, so you don't need to worry about your school. It'll save you from Noreen's cooking, too."

"In that case I will come," laughed Elizabeth. Fiddksticks to Olive and her jealousy. She couldn't organise her own life to suit other people's moods and there were more important matters to be concerned about. If Olive wanted to be unfriendly, let her be. There was always Noreen with her slap-happy ways, and Louise.

After tea she went down to the stables again, and at Noreen's prompting, she wore her slacks. The children were just inside the yard, clustered around Steve. One of them obviously noticed her approach, for they all looked in her direction and the conversation ended immediately. They mounted their bicycles and pedalled away along a sandy track, followed by a dark brown dog. With the exception of Julie, who was still painfully shy, they all gave a half-hearted wave to Elizabeth. They plainly intended to avoid her company as much as possible.

"How did your first day go?" asked Steve as she reached the gate.

"Very well, thank you. Have the children been telling you about it?"

"Not they. Brian had found a large black beetle and they were talking about that."

"Is he particularly interested in that kind of thing?"

"They all seem to be. Whenever they find anything new they bring it down here." Steve looked pensively at the track along which the children had gone. "I suppose there's no one else to show their treasures to. Mark's always busy and none of the others bother much with them."

Elizabeth had nothing to say to that. Steve had summed up the children's problem quite clearly. Everybody at the ranch was too busy to bother about them. On the other hand, it seemed rather odd that they had caused governess to leave. She would have expected them to welcome anybody who paid attention to them.

"You've been here for a long time, haven't you, Steve?"

"Four years and a bit."

"Mark was telling me today that they gave their governess a lot of trouble."

"Yeah, they did. One didn't last a week."

"I'm wondering why."

Steve laughed. "Because they're lazy, of course. It takes ages to recruit new staff. Without a governess all they did was School of the Air, then fill in the answers on the correspondence sheets." He shook his head. "I don't suppose they bothered whether the answers were correct or not. After that they just went out and enjoyed themselves for the rest of the day."

No wonder they had resented her arrival. It had curtailed their freedom. Now they were being polite and co-operative because they had been presented with an ultimatum — either work well for her, or leave home and go to boarding school where they would have even less freedom. How long would it be before they lost their fear of upsetting her and behaved naturally?

"I see you've got your slacks on today," said Steve, breaking into her thoughts. "Going to try your skill at riding?"

"I'm not sure." Elizabeth turned to look at the horses, staring solemnly at her from the far side of the yard. "Noreen tried to persuade me."

"There's nothing to it. I'll saddle William for you. He's a really staid old thing."

Elizabeth returned to the ranch bubbling over with enthusiasm about her first ride and a close-up view of a dingo.

"The folk at the station would have a fit if they knew I was feeding a dingo," Steve had said. "But I look at it this way; if he has enough to eat here, he won't go hunting their stock."

Noreen listened complacently, continuing her work without any fuss, and as Elizabeth guessed, the dinner was good despite all the adverse comments. The others dispersed after the meal, but she stayed behind to help Louise and Noreen to tidy up.

"What happened to Mark this evening?" asked Elizabeth. "Didn't he want any dinner?"

"He decided he ought to eat with the kids," answered Noreen. "He sees little enough of them as it is."

Elizabeth thought how little she had seen of the children since Saturday. They never seemed to be about. "Don't they eat with him usually?"

"No, Mark doesn't want them in the dining-room with the tourists." Noreen lifted a gravy dish that had been left full of water to soak. "Mind out of the way while I empty this."

"You mean they nearly always have their meals by themselves?"

"There's no alternative," said Louise. "Annie won't have the kids in the kitchen."

Elizabeth restrained herself from saying more. She felt very strongly about the children being left to their own devices so much, particularly at meal times, but she must not gossip behind Mark's back. Next time she had the opportunity to talk privately with him she would raise the problem, but she must be very diplomatic about the whole affair, and have some kind of solution to suggest. It would be so easy to sound too critical, and she had the feeling that she had shown more than enough disapproval of his methods during their discussion in the schoolroom that afternoon.

CHAPTER NINE

THE CHILDREN were neatly dressed again the following morning and school began on a fairly even note, but Elizabeth discovered that Brian was even weaker in mathematics than she had suspected.

"How did you do this one, Brian?" she asked, pointing to the third sum.

"I took that away from that, then that away from that."

"Oh dear, they tricked you with the signs. They're not all subtraction you know."

"Oh."

"You should really have guessed there was something wrong with that. You can't subtract when you have three rows of figures."

Brian looked down at the paper again, shrugged and then stared at her defiantly. "Why don't you just go ahead and say it?" he demanded.

"Say what?"

"I'm dumb."

Elizabeth was shocked by his reaction. "You're not dumb, Brian." He made a peculiar sound of scorn and disbelief and she went on as convincingly as possible. "You can do all kinds of clever things. I know you're a bit out of practice with maths, but that's understandable after being on holiday all these weeks."

"Patricia said I was dumb."

"She was our last governess," Margaret put in. She had been listening to the exchange with avid interest. "She was always saying he was dumb. Sometimes she said we all were."

"She didn't really mean that," said Elizabeth, hoping this was not going to lead to an awkward discussion. "She'd only say it because she was feeling impatient at the time."

"She did mean it," said Brian. "And she was right, too. The papers always came back marked wrong."

"No, they didn't. Only the last three or four weeks when you didn't have a governess to help."

"I never got them right before. Only she used to change them and I copied them out with the right answer on the proper paper.

Elizabeth hastily pulled a fresh sheet of paper forward and began to write figures on it to fill in time until she felt ready to speak again. She had never dreamed that the situation had been so appalling, and she was quite certain that Mark had not realised.

"Dad thinks I'm dumb, too," went on Brian. He seemed determined to convince her of his uselessness. "He said so."

Elizabeth sighed and laid her pencil down. "You must have done something silly and made him cross. People don't really mean what they say when they're cross."

"And he said he'd got a special teacher, and he said if I couldn't learn anything then I'd have to go away to school."

"I suppose I'm the special teacher," answered Elizabeth calmly and smiled at him. "You know, the only special thing about me is that I used to teach a lot of girls and boys all at once, instead of just a few like you. Can you imagine forty-five or fifty children all making the same mistakes as you?"

"Did they?" asked Brian in surprise.

"Well, of course. Everybody makes mistakes when they're learning something new. If they knew how to do everything they wouldn't need to go to school, would they?"

"I suppose not," mumbled Brian. The idea of other children having difficulties had apparently never occurred to him.

"Don't you worry, Brian. You're not stupid and your father knows it. That's why he expects you to do a lot better. But he'll be surprised when you show him how quickly you can do it."

Brian seemed to lose some of his tension after that episode, and even Margaret looked less sullen. Julie was still shy and hardly spoke a word all day, but Elizabeth felt light-hearted as they scampered out that afternoon. She was certain she had overcome the first hurdle and matters would improve rapidly. The barbecue had suddenly become an event to look forward to, and she hummed gaily to herself as she sauntered across to her cabin.

There were five tourists in the party that had arrived by air, middle-aged, talkative Americans. Elizabeth settled herself into a seat at the back of the battered vehicle that Mark used for small groups, responding gaily to Olive's forced smile of greeting. Noreen had confided to her that after years of practice Mark was perfectly capable of handling everything by himself, but Olive found these occasions ideal for making herself seem indispensable.

"If Mark hasn't realised by now that she's got designs on him, he'd better start waking up," she had laughed. "She only makes herself useful when he's around to notice."

They drove for over an hour, then Mark drew up in a narrow gulley and the tourists scrambled out to take photographs and explore. Elizabeth joined them and soon found herself chatting readily. What a contrast to her highly strung and self-conscious state of a few weeks ago. She had begun to give up hope of ever regaining her former poise and marvelled that only a few days in these surroundings could have wrought such a change.

When they hurried back towards a vantage spot to watch the effect of the sunset, Mark immediately noticed the difference in Elizabeth.

"You're looking extremely fit," he told her. "What did I say about this being an ideal place for you?"

94

"You were right," agreed Elizabeth. "I haven't felt as well as this for months."

The tourists noisily admired the beauties of the sunset as the colours glowed, changed and faded on the sheer rock face before them. Dusk fell swiftly when the display ended and they returned to the vehicle where Olive was preparing the barbecue. With the enthusiasm of small boys the three men in the American party collected wood for a second fire to sit around.

In their exuberance they all bundled their collection of dead branches onto the new fire. The dry material caught alight at once, throwing sparks into the air and sending up long tendrils of flame. Elizabeth moved back, looking for a place to sit outside that circle of light. She found a smooth log that had obviously been set there to serve as a seat, but the flickering glow on the surrounding rocks unnerved her. She swivelled around and stared into the darkness, her hands clenched together. Her forehead was clammy with sweat and her appetite had vanished.

Mark had turned in annoyance when the sudden blaze attracted his attention. Certain types of tourists would always start another fire when he was occupied with something else. They always made them far too large wasting fuel that was valuable in that dry area, and ruining any chance of seeing wild life. He made a gesture of exasperation to Olive, then resumed his task of cooking meat. No point in making a fuss. It was too late to save the wood for encourage animals to come closer.

He called out that the rare steaks were ready and the tourists gradually collected their portions as they were cooked the way they liked. He had expected Elizabeth with her new-found confidence to join them, but she had not come forward by the time Olive had cooked two more rare steaks for themselves. He filled a second plate, told Olive to keep the tourists company and moved off in search of Elizabeth.

She was hunched on the log that he and Steve had brought back from the cattle station two seasons ago, and he realised with a pang that she had lost her vitality. Even in the gloom it was clear that she had reverted to the tense condition she had been in when he first set eyes on her.

"I've brought your dinner over," he said hesitantly.

There was a pause while Elizabeth struggled to gain control of herself. "Thank you. But I'm afraid I'm not hungry after all."

Mark looked down at her uncertainly, then back at the party of tourists. In the glare of the flames he could see them plainly, some eating with their fingers as they chatted and joked. As he turned back to Elizabeth the cause of her sudden change of mood became obvious.

"It's the fire that's upset you, isn't it?"

She made no reply and he stepped over the log to

sit beside her. "I'm sorry. They lit it before I realised what they were up to, but I'd have taken more care if I'd known it would bother you."

"It's all right," she managed to say.

"I'll put it out."

Elizabeth drew herself up a little. "No, don't do that. I wouldn't want to cause any…"For a moment she was lost for words. "I don't want to attract any attention," she blurted at last.

"I can do it without that. There are plenty of reasons for not wanting a big fire in the bush."

"I'd prefer you not to."

Mark glanced back at the dancing flames. "It'll burn down soon anyway. I'll tell them not to waste any more fuel on it." He held a plate out and although her first reaction was to reject it, she took it from him.

"Thank you."

"Would you like me to stay here for a while?"

"No thank you, I shall be all right now. The other people will want you there."

"Try to eat a little. Shall I tell them you're planning lessons for composing poetry or something?"

"Perhaps you'd better say I'm feeling the heat. I don't suppose I'll be the best of company on the way back."

The tourists were full of sympathy when Elizabeth eventually rejoined them. She told them that she had felt a little faint but had fully recovered, and kept a grip on her composure during the journey to the ranch.

"Can I get you anything?" asked Mark softly, as he helped her down from the vehicle.

Elizabeth pulled her hand away from his. "No, thank you. Don't worry. I'm perfectly all right now."

Olive was watching from a short distance and she suddenly stepped forward, offering to help Elizabeth back to her cabin. She declined politely, repeating that she felt better, and the tourists wished her a hearty good night before going into the bar for more jollity. Elizabeth walked down the gritty path, flashing her torch carefully ahead to make sure no unwelcome creatures lay in wait for her. She had learned to accept the geckoes, for they really did seem harmless and quite beautiful as Steve had said, but she was still nervous about meeting some of the other horrible creatures she had heard about.

She locked her door and leaned against it for several moments, then crossed to the bed and curled up on it miserably. After the pleasant hour of talking and laughing with the tourists, the sudden attack brought on by the sight of that fire had been doubly cruel. She had begun to believe that she was on the mend at last, but disillusionment had followed quickly. She would never be rid of the haunting scenes of the past. She huddled into a tighter ball and tears slid down her cheeks.

Annie Fenn was the first one to spot the dark rings beneath her eyes the next morning.

"The afternoon out didn't do you much good."

Elizabeth tried to pass the affair over with nonchalance. "I must have overdone things a little. Perhaps I shouldn't have tried to keep up with everybody before I was properly acclimatised."

"You're not looking so good even now," said Louise, pouring cereal into a row of dishes.

"I didn't sleep very well, but I'm all right otherwise."

Annie turned back to the stove. "A place like this is no use for weak specimens," she muttered audibly. "Mark should have known what would happen."

Elizabeth's paleness changed to scarlet and Louise winked at her as a sign that she should take no notice of the remark. "Some people know more about other people's jobs than their own," she said.

Mark entered the kitchen to check that everything was running smoothly, but on catching sight of Elizabeth he broke off what he was about to say.

"You'd better take the day off," he told her.

"That's not necessary," she answered.

"The kids have managed before. They can do it again. Margaret will keep an eye on things."

The idea of permitting the children to continue in the former slip-shod method prodded Elizabeth into action. She drew herself up with dignity. "I think I am the best person to judge whether or not I am capable of taking a class."

She had never spoken so boldly to him before. Mark stared in surprise then shrugged his shoulders.

"It's up to you, of course. But please take care."

"I shall. I have no intention of overdoing it, so none of you need worry about complications setting in."

Even Annie seemed to accept the hint that the subject should be closed. Nobody referred to her health again and she ate her usual light breakfast in a calmer frame of mind. When she set off across the wide expanse of sun-baked earth at the back of the building she was feeling in complete control of herself, and she greeted the children quite naturally.

As always, Pauline was the most out-going of them all. She leaned against Elizabeth's table and gazed earnestly into her face.

"Dad said we've got to be very quiet this morning."

"Did he?"

"Yes. He said you weren't feeling very well last night."

"No, as a matter of fact I wasn't. But that was last night. I'm feeling well again now."

"I'm glad. It wouldn't have been as nice in here by ourselves. Does that mean we don't have to be quiet now?"

Elizabeth laughed. "Not specially quiet, anyway. But you mustn't be too noisy or you'll get nothing done."

When School of the Air was over they always had a short break, but instead of rushing out to play this morning, Carl lingered.

"Auntie Rose is coming back today with the new baby."

"Auntie Rose?" That must be Steve's wife. "Oh, how exciting."

"She's coming on the plane. We're all going to see her this afternoon."

"That will be nice."

"Are you coming?" asked Pauline from the doorway.

Elizabeth gripped the edge of her table as another wave of nausea swept over her. She could not face that today, not after yesterday's episode. "No, not today," she told them.

"Why not?" asked Carl.

Elizabeth sought quickly for an excuse that would satisfy them. "Auntie Rose will have lots of visitors today, so she won't want to meet anybody new just yet. Besides, I'm not going out in the sun today."

The plane arrived just after Elizabeth entered the kitchen for lunch. Everybody had been listening for the engines and talk burst out as the aircraft zoomed to a landing somewhere beyond the stables.

"Noreen's gone with Mark to meet her," said Louise enviously. "I bet Rose is dying to show the baby off."

"Pity the aircraft always arrives when we're stuck here serving lunch," said Olive.

"There is such a thing as a crowd," declared Annie.

"Anyone'd think the baby's only going to be here

for two minutes."

"It would be nice to be there and welcome her though, wouldn't it?" sighed Louise. "What do you think, Elizabeth?"

"It would be nice," agreed Elizabeth. From her level tone nobody could be aware of the turmoil raging inside her. "But I think she and Steve should have a chance to be alone for a while."

Olive seemed to take that as criticism. "Mark and Noreen are only going to see them at the airstrip," she retorted. "They'll have time enough to be alone."

"We're all going down there this afternoon, or this evening," said Louise. "You coming, Elizabeth?"

Once again Elizabeth forced herself to speak calmly. "No, thank you. I think Rose should see all her friends before meeting anybody new."

"Rose isn't shy. She'll take to you right away."

"Another day," answered Elizabeth. "I think I'd better stay after school, just to be on the safe side."

Everybody was too engrossed in events to notice how little she ate, and she was able to slip away early without an elaborate excuse. She went down to her cabin to fill in time until school was due to begin again, and washed a few garments to keep her hands occupied. Soon she would have to meet Rose and admire the new baby. There was no escape from that. But not yet. In a day or two, but not yet.

CHAPTER TEN

ON SATURDAY morning Elizabeth steeled herself to make a visit to Steve's house. That could not be evaded any longer. As it was, people might have noticed that she seemed unwilling to go, and Steve would feel offended if she did not make an appearance soon. She planned to walk down just after lunch, when everybody at the ranch would be fully occupied and unable to accompany her.

Steve was relaxing in the lounge and he saw her crossing the front garden. "So here you are," he said, opening the screen door for her. "Come on in. We were beginning to wonder when you would show up."

"I hope you didn't think I was rude, not coming to meet your wife before this."

"Course not. You've been a bit crook, I heard. How're you feeling now?"

"I'm very well, thank you."

"You chose the hottest part of the day to come down here."

"It's not really far, and I'm quite fit again now."

"Glad to hear it. Sit down." Steve motioned to a tubular easy chair and raised his voice. "Rose,

Elizabeth is here."

"I know, I heard. I'm just fixing this."

Rose left the kitchen almost immediately and smiled a welcome at her visitor as she came through the doorway She paid more attention to her appearance than the other women in the area, and made an attractive sight in her bright yellow and orange floral dress. Although she wore no make-up her complexion was well cared for, and she had obviously visited a hairdressing salon before leaving town. Steve put his arm proudly around her waist and made the introductions.

"I've heard a lot about you," said Rose. "Have you settled in well?"

"Yes, thank you."

They exchanged small talk for several minutes and Steve began to lose patience. "Don't you want to see the baby?" he demanded.

"I'd love to. But don't risk waking her up."

"Not a chance." Steve jerked his head towards the passage. "This way."

The baby was sleeping contentedly, lying on her right side under a light covering. Elizabeth stared down at her, remembering the kind of phrases that pleased new parents. The moment was not as painful as she had feared.

"We're going to call her Barbara," said Rose. "After Steve's mother."

At last they moved back to the lounge and some of Elizabeth's tension left her. Rose produced three icy drinks made from fresh lemons and conversation became less stilted.

"I'm going down to check that engine," said Steve suddenly. He stood up and stretched leisurely. "Don't go Elizabeth. I'll be back soon and I'll drive you up to the ranch. Save you the walk"

"Oh, but…"

"Keep Rose company for a bit. She's missing all those other mothers in the ward."

"I'd like you to stay," said Rose. "As long as you have nothing more important to do."

"Of course I haven't."

Rose waved her husband off from the doorstep, then turned and regarded Elizabeth thoughtfully.

"You don't seem very much at ease. I hope they're treating you properly up at the ranch."

"Yes, they are. It's just that I'm not good at meeting new people."

"I don't suppose meeting Annie was any fun then." Rose laughed and went back to her chair. She was as amiable as Noreen, but in a much more ladylike way. "If you think I'm likely to be jealous because you went out with Steve two days running — forget it. I'm not that way inclined, and I know Steve."

Elizabeth smiled back. The fact that Steve's wife might be jealous of those occasions had not occurred to her before. "I suppose he told you that he was trying to educate me on the subject of insects and so forth."

Rose laughed again. "He hasn't had such an appreciative audience for ages. He loves to talk about nature. I hope you felt more confident afterwards."

"Yes, I did. I still don't like creepy-crawlers, but I don't think I'll scream the place down if I see one now."

"Good." Rose glanced towards her empty glass, then her face became more serious and she leaned forward. "I don't think Olive is over-fond of you, is she?"

"No, she isn't. But she's not causing any unpleasantness."

"Just watch out, that's all. She took great pains to inform me about your outings with Steve."

"Oh."

"Don't worry. I'd already heard all about them, and even if I hadn't, it would take more than that kind of tittle-tattle to upset me. So you can relax, make yourself at home, and take any more nature lessons that you fancy." Rose picked up her glass, then seemed to change her mind and put it down again. "Look, Elizabeth, I've heard that you've been very ill, following some kind of accident."

Elizabeth nodded and the other woman went on quietly. "I used to be a nurse. I don't suppose you want to talk about it, but I assume you had some kind of break-down." Elizabeth nodded again and Rose smiled gently. "I'm not going to pry. But I just wanted to tell you that if you get the feeling that things are getting on top of you any time, you can drop in here. I'll help in any way I can."

"Thank you," muttered Elizabeth.

"Having got all that over, how about another lemon drink?"

By the time Steve returned they were chatting like old friends and he grinned with relief. People usually took to Rose easily and he had been puzzled when Elizabeth had not done so.

"Bill and Lesley are coming over from the station this evening," he said. "How about you coming down to meet them?"

"Oh, I don't know..." Elizabeth quailed at the thought of more company that day.

"It's a great idea," said Rose, nodding enthusiastically "Do come, Elizabeth. They'll want to meet you, and this will be a great opportunity to get it over with. While they're so interested in the baby you won't be the centre of attraction."

"You have a point there," agreed Elizabeth. She took a deep breath and decided to accept. Rose was right, it would be the easiest way to meet the other people, even though she would have to be in close proximity to the baby again so soon.

The evening passed better than she had hoped. The couple from the cattle station were hearty, down to earth people who instantly made her feel like one of the group. Lesley was so captivated by the baby, wanting to handle her when she awakened, that Elizabeth was able to slip away on the pretext that she had had her chance to do all that during the afternoon. She was jolted for a moment when Bill wanted to add spirits to her soft drink, but Rose rushed to her aid, telling him that she was still under doctor's orders and not permitted to drink alcohol. Elizabeth smiled at her gratefully. The ex-nurse had the unusual knack of knowing what was needed in moments of stress, and gave promise of being a staunch friend.

Bill and Lesley dropped her off at the ranch on their way back to the station. It was past midnight, far later than she had stayed out for almost two years, and she slept late the next morning. She skipped breakfast, but lingered in the kitchen after lunch to tell the others about her social evening. Olive was disgruntled because nobody else had been invited, but Louise and Noreen were keen to hear the latest gossip.

Mark called to Elizabeth as she passed the dining-room on her way back to the cabin. He hurried outside and smiled down at her, hands thrust into the pockets of his shorts.

"You're looking fitter again now, I'm pleased to say. I hear you went out to Steve's place last night."

"Yes, I met Bill and Lesley."

"I'm glad to hear it. I don't want you to stay in you own quarters all the time, feeling neglected."

"I don't feel neglected at all," she answered.

"I hope not. But Noreen tells me you don't appear very often. You seem to spend a lot of time alone."

Elizabeth could not resist a sly dig. "You gave me the end cabin so that I could be quiet, didn't you?"

He laughed at that. "Yes, I did. But don't hibernate there. I've been feeling a bit guilty, not keeping in touch with you and helping you to settle in, but somehow I can't find enough hours in a day when tourists are around."

"I know how it is. I've been very busy myself. This is only my second week here after all."

"How are the kids coming along? Any problems?"

"They're catching up on their weak points very quickly." Elizabeth hesitated. This hardly seemed an ideal time to raise the subject of the children's meals, but days might pass before they had an opportunity of speaking privately again.

"What's the trouble then?" asked Mark. "Something's bothering you."

"It's not exactly bothering me. It's just something I thought I ought to mention."

Elizabeth went on to talk of the children's home life, and how they seemed to be bringing themselves up. As she spoke, a solution occurred to her, but she paused to allow him to comment first. Mark's smile had faded and his shoulder sagged a little.

"You're right, of course. They've been left even more than usual this season, what with Annie being in the kitchen and Rose having a baby. I don't know what to do about it. I could take on more staff, I suppose, but it's not easy to get the right people, as

I've said before."

"It's quite simple. I'll have my lunch and dinner with them."

Mark regarded her solemnly, thought for a moment, then shook his head. "No, that won't do. You weren't employed as a nursemaid. You need a rest from kids outside school hours."

"There'll be plenty of time for that. They don't take long over lunch, and we can get away from each other for three or four hours between school and dinner."

"I can't ask you to do it."

"You're not asking — I'm offering." The more she thought of it, the more the idea appealed to Elizabeth. "It will be better for me in many ways. I can get to know the children better, and I won't feel that I'm a nuisance."

"Has anybody been making you feel uncomfortable?" asked Mark sharply.

"No, of course not. It's just my own attitude. I feel awkward sitting there doing nothing when all the others are so busy."

Mark wavered. "You could give it a go, I suppose. But not every day. You'll end up as a complete recluse if you're not careful."

Elizabeth smiled. "I shall be finished long before the others have cleared up in the kitchen. And of course, I shan't go when you have the chance to be with them. I only hope the children won't object to me being there."

"They'd better not," he retorted. His face became stern, as it always did when he thought of the children's less attractive behaviour, then he brightened. "They won't. I think they've taken to you, even though they haven't said much."

Mark promised to arrange for her meals to be sent across the next day and Elizabeth turned to go. A slight movement caught her eye and she looked again at the dining-room window. The curtain was now still, but a vague shape was visible in the background. Olive, of course, spying on her chosen quarry and wondering what the long discussion was about. Elizabeth's amusement battled with indignation. Olive must be unsure of herself to worry every time Mark spoke to another female. Useless to inform her that she was wasting her time in this case. She would never believe that Elizabeth had no intention of becoming a rival for his attention.

Before lessons started the next day, Elizabeth mentioned that she would be taking some of her meals at the house. Pauline looked pleased and Carl announced that Mark had already explained. The other three stared at her glumly, then Margaret spoke up.

"What are we supposed to learn?"

"You won't be learning anything. We only do school-work during school hours."

"Why are you coming then? None of the others ever did."

"I thought it would be nice to have company, and

it would make a change for you."

The children scurried through lunch to escape as rapidly as possible, and were constrained at dinner. Margaret was on edge, thinking that their teacher had come to supervise table manners. She kicked Carl to remind him not to use his fingers, and scowled at Julie when she splashed gravy onto the cloth. Elizabeth pretended not to notice how awkward they all were. Except for the few occasions when their father joined them, they probably ignored most of the niceties of table behaviour. She tried to act naturally, breaking the silence every now and again with an amusing anecdote about other children she had known.

Margaret collected the dishes together, telling Elizabeth that they took turns at washing them.

"What time are you all supposed to be in bed?" asked Elizabeth.

Margaret indicated the three youngest. "They're supposed to go after we've tidied up. They've had their showers."

"Well, if everything is tidied up quickly and they hurry up and get undressed, I'll tell them a story before I go."

Pauline clasped her hands together in delight, her eyes shining with excitement. "A story! Are you really going to tell us a story?"

"Yes, if you hurry up."

Julie said nothing, but her enthusiasm was plain. She gathered up a pile of dessert plates and almost ran into the kitchen, knocking down a tin of pan scourer as she fumbled hastily for the washing-up liquid. Carl hastened after her to help and Margaret stared rebelliously at Elizabeth.

"Where's the story going to be?"

"I haven't decided yet. Where does everybody sleep?"

"Carl and Brian there. Pauline and Julie there. And I sleep out there." Margaret wafted one arm in the general direction of the rooms.

"We could have it in the girls' bedroom then."

"Does everybody have to come?"

"No, of course not. It will be a story for young children, but anybody who wants to can come."

Elizabeth suspected that Brian wanted to join the younger children, but eventually he followed Margaret's lead and stayed away. The other three sat cross-legged on Pauline's bed in their pyjamas and an argument broke off almost immediately between Pauline, who wanted The Three Bears, and Carl who wanted a new story. Elizabeth smiled at Julie, who had not taken part.

"What do you want Julie? A new story or one we've had in school?"

Julie bit her lip and finally made one of her few brief speeches. "A new one please," she whispered.

Elizabeth told them The Sleeping Beauty and they were delighted.

"That's even nicer than The Three Bears," said Pauline.

"Serve you right if you'd missed it," retorted Carl.

Elizabeth laughed and pushed her chair back into the corner. "You can choose a story tomorrow, Carl, and Pauline the day after."

"Oh, goodie, goodie." The children rolled backwards, kicking their feet in the air, and Pauline suddenly bounced off the bed.

"I'm glad you came here, Miss Gaunt. We've never had a story at bed-time before."

"We never had any stories," added Carl. "Except those on the school sheets. Margaret usually read those for us. And she's a rotten reader."

114

CHAPTER ELEVEN

THE STORIES at bed-time did more to win the children's friendship than anything Elizabeth had thought of so far. Brian came into the bedroom for the third story and Margaret stayed just beyond the open door so that she could hear. Without doubt she would join the group when her pride allowed. Victory seemed close when Elizabeth told them that their dog, Bess, could stay in the schoolroom so long as she was quiet and they did not play with her.

The red puppy had taken to waiting for Elizabeth outside the bungalow, and they gradually drifted into a routine. Rufus dozed on the tiled floor in her bathroom while she prepared lessons, and when the day became cooler she took him for a walk. On one of these outings Elizabeth noticed large footprints and followed the trail until she saw Charles crouched over some kind of apparatus beside an ant-hill. Rufus bounded up to greet him and Charles rose, revealing a camera and tripod.

"Don't knock that over, you little devil," he said, patting the puppy good-naturedly and then trying to make him sit. "Hello, Elizabeth."

"Hello, Charles. I hope Rufus hasn't done any

harm."

"No, I haven't started yet. I was only measuring up." Charles watched the puppy as it sniffed at the tripod and then the ant-hill, decided there was nothing interesting about either, and loped across to a spiky tussock. "I'm making a film about ants. Steve lent me a book about them and I got really interested. You'll be able to see inside this hill when I knock a piece off. After I've filmed it I'm going to look for a really good mulga ants' nest. Do you want to come along?"

"Are you sure Rufus won't get in the way?"

"No, he'll be all right. And you can keep a hold on him if he gets too nosey."

As they rambled about together, Charles described ants and their habits, speaking eloquently as always. Elizabeth became engrossed and he went on to tell her about other insects he was studying with Steve's help. Her heart was light as they walked back towards the ranch, laughing at the puppy's antics. Everything seemed to be running smoothly now, and a little more time spent with Steve and Charles would surely overcome her last qualms about creeping things.

On Sunday she joined the tourists for a full day trip, and during a quiet moment Mark stopped to tell her how much the children enjoyed the extra attention they had received lately. His praise of her abilities grew effusive and, as usual when conversation became personal, she blushed. Olive watched from her position at the side of the coach where she was preparing the barbecue, her expression growing icier. Elizabeth automatically glanced in her direction and at the sight of that grim look tried to edge away from Mark. It would never do to upset Olive to the extent where the tourists noticed a stormy atmosphere. In her jealousy she was quite oblivious to onlookers, and she was making no attempt to disguise her hostility.

"I'll give Olive a hand," she told Mark, as an excuse to end the talk.

Mark readily agreed to that suggestion and accompanied her to the folding table, but Olive refused any help and barely camouflaged the surly tone in her voice.

"You'll only get in the way. This table isn't big enough for people who don't know the routine, and George'll be over in a minute."

The rebuff came as no surprise to Elizabeth and she smiled as she strolled away to rejoin the tourists. In comparison with Annie Fenn, Olive's attempts to squelch her ego were very mild.

Elizabeth saw nothing of the children that day, but they all seemed content to start school again the next morning. Brian completed his mathematics without a single mistake, and Margaret read aloud with far less hesitation than usual. Elizabeth was congratulating herself on her achievements when she opened the small drawer in her table and reached inside for a poetry book. She only just managed to change a scream into a gasp, and slammed the drawer sharply. The five children stared at her as she sank onto the chair, fighting to keep control over herself.

"What's the matter, Miss Gaunt?" asked Pauline.

Elizabeth took a deep breath. It was ridiculous to be afraid of a mere insect, no matter how ugly it seemed to be. Besides, she had convinced herself only the other day that she need not be afraid of anything she might come across. She must be cautious about red backs, of course, but this was no such thing.

"There's a spider in the drawer," she said.

"What kind?" asked Carl.

"I don't know yet." Elizabeth forced herself to open the drawer slowly, ready to dodge if the creature jumped. The spider crouched in the front right hand corner, looking just as large as she had imagined at first sight. One leg moved slightly, as if to prove it was alive.

"It's a big black one," she announced, sliding the drawer shut again. "I wonder how it got there?"

"Has it made a web?" asked Carl.

"I don't think so." Elizabeth looked around at her pupils. Now that she had recovered from the shock her suspicions were rising. The inside of such a well-fitting drawer seemed an odd place to find a spider of that size. "Who put it there?"

The children looked at each other as if they were puzzled and stared back at her.

"Nobody did, Miss Gaunt," said Pauline.

"I'm quite sure somebody did. Well, you've had your joke, and it worked. You gave me a fright. Who's going to take it away?"

"I will," said Carl, eager as always for some unusual activity.

"Can I see it?" asked Brian.

"Did you put it there, Brian?"

"No, Miss Gaunt. Honest. Can I see it?"

Her assent was taken to include everybody and they all crowded around the table. Brian slid the drawer open, wary of injuring the creature, and gave a cry of delight.

"Oh, Miss Gaunt! It's beaut! I've never seen one as big as that. Can I have it?"

His excitement was so intense there was no doubting that he had never seen the spider before. The others battled for a view and sounded almost as surprised and thrilled.

Only Margaret held herself a little aloof and gazed without comment.

"Did you put it there. Margaret?" asked Elizabeth.

"No, Miss Gaunt." The girl stared back at her as if daring her to argue the point, then added, "If I'd seen that anywhere I'd have given it to Steve."

"Can I go and get something to put it in?" asked Brian.

"Yes, of course."

Brian rushed away to another part of the house,

returning seconds later with an empty jam jar, and Elizabeth watched over the children's heads as he caught the spider gently. "Isn't it terrific, Miss Gaunt?"

Elizabeth tried to show some enthusiasm. "It's certainly very big. Do you know what kind it is?"

"It looks like a tarantula with those hairy legs, doesn't it? But I don't think we have any of those up here."

"Well, I expect Steve will be able to tell you all about it. Put it somewhere safe and then we'll get on with some work."

The excitement soon wore off and the children continued their lessons in the normal way, but Elizabeth could not forget the incident and she examined the table carefully when they had left the room at lunchtime. As she had suspected the drawer fitted snugly on all sides. There seemed to be no inducement for a fat, hairy spider to force a way in. Elizabeth sighed. Apparently her pupils were not honest. One of them at least could look her in the eye and tell a lie without showing any signs of confusion or embarrassment.

She was still feeling unsettled when school was over, but the customary walk with Rufus in the peace of the bush had a soothing effect. She told the children a story after dinner, tucked the three youngest into bed and went across to the kitchen for a chat with the rest of the staff. Noreen was washing dishes at the sink, singing boisterously out of tune, while Annie was sitting back with a cup of tea, enjoying her time off and watching the others work.

"Hi, Elizabeth. Nice of you to visit the slaves." Noreen yanked the plug out of the sink and turned to Elizabeth with a mischievous grin. "Brian showed me a massive spider today."

Elizabeth chuckled. "He'll probably show it to everybody he can find. He's very proud of it."

Olive placed a loaded tray on a side table and watched Elizabeth with amused malice. "Were you scared?" she asked.

Elizabeth shrugged. "It certainly made me jump when I first saw it. But I didn't faint or anything, if that's what you mean."

"Where was it?" asked Annie.

"In my drawer at school."

"Funny that it should choose your drawer out of all of them."

"Do you think it was planted?" asked Noreen.

"I wouldn't be at all surprised," answered Elizabeth lightly. "It's the kind of trick children get up to, especially boys.

"They're back to their old ways then," sniffed Annie. "In the next week or so you'll find out what you've let yourself in for. Mark'll be sorry in the end. He should send them for some proper discipline now, before they get too old for it."

Elizabeth turned away to hide the angry flush that darted up her neck and face. "I'll give you a hand with the cutlery if you like, Noreen."

"I thought you'd never get around to offering."
Noreen was not the type to decline help from any
quarter and she hastily tossed a tea towel to
Elizabeth. "All those in the cans are clean. They just
need drying."

The next time George drove back from town he
brought a large carton for Elizabeth. She realised that
the books had come and had the box carried over to
the schoolroom, but she would not allow the children
to investigate until School of the Air was over. As
soon as the radio session ended they jumped up,
begging her to let them open the box instead of
having play time. She gave permission with a laugh
and they all jostled for position, each hoping to be
the first to see the contents.

"Ooh, there's lots of books," exclaimed Pauline,
grabbing the nearest one. "Can I have this one?"

"That's too old for you," retorted Margaret. "You
won't be able to read it."

"You'll read it to me, won't you, Miss Gaunt?"

"You look at some of the others," laughed
Elizabeth.

"I'm sure you'll find one that you can read
yourself. Be careful with them, though."

They sorted through the collection of books,
putting some aside instantly and stopping to examine
others more closely. Brian found an illustrated
encyclopaedia and immediately lost interest in the
remainder, while Margaret became entranced by
pictures of horses. Julie was flushed with

excitement, clutching a book in each hand and trying to make up her mind which one to look at first. Elizabeth watched in amusement as she changed her mind and peered into the box again.

"There's another parcel in there, Miss Gaunt."

"Is there really? Let me see." Elizabeth pulled out a heavy packet with an envelope stuck to the outside. "There's a letter for me, too."

She read the first few lines, then put the letter back in the envelope for a more peaceful time.

"Open the parcel," said Pauline. "Please," she added, remembering how strict their teacher had been about that word lately. "We want to see what you've got."

"It's not for me. It's for all of you."

"For us?" gasped Pauline.

Carl felt the edges of the packet. "It's not books."

"No, this is different. It's a present from my brother and his wife." Elizabeth smiled at the ring of happy faces. "I think Margaret should open this. She's always letting the rest of you do the exciting things."

Jean had sent five boxes of paints, each one individually wrapped and marked with a name in red ink. The children tore the paper off and opened the boxes with sighs and exclamations of joy.

"Mine's got two brushes," cried Pauline.

"So's mine," answered Brian. "Look, they all have."

"Can we try them now? Please, Miss Gaunt," said

Carl.

Elizabeth had never seen a group of children so excited about opening a parcel, which seemed odd considering how prosperous the family appeared to be. Their enthusiasm was so great she decided to shelve the timetable and have an art lesson. "Yes, you may use them now," she answered. "I'll get some paper while you bring the water."

"What shall I paint, Miss Gaunt?" asked Pauline, wriggling on her chair.

"Anything you like. Your house, perhaps, or the canyon at sunset."

Four of them started immediately, but Margaret hovered uncertainly near her table. "May I go outside to do mine?" she asked at last.

"Won't you find that a bit awkward with water and everything?"

"No, I'll manage fine. I'll only go as far as the garden."

"All right," agreed Elizabeth. "This does seem to be a special day, doesn't it? But be careful. Remember how that earth stains your clothes if you get wet."

In their usual slap-happy way, Carl and Pauline finished two highly coloured pictures each while Julie and Brian laboured over one. Lunchtime was drawing close so Elizabeth went outside to find Margaret. She was sitting on the grass near the croton bushes, frowning at a sheet of paper propped up in front of her. Elizabeth stooped to see it and drew her breath in sharply.

"Margaret! That's beautiful!"

"Do you really think so?" Margaret looked up doubtfully as if suspecting her teacher's motives, and Elizabeth found herself sinking down onto the grass for a closer inspection. The pale blue flower was well-proportioned, the delicate colours of the petals and leaves applied with an artistic touch.

"Did you paint this from memory?" she asked.

"No, there's one in the garden. Look, right here."

Margaret pointed out a tiny plant barely three inches high, and Elizabeth marvelled again at her prowess.

"It's really beautiful, Margaret. How did you learn to paint so well?"

"I can only paint flowers and leaves and things."

"Did somebody teach you?"

"Mrs. Snowdon. She painted wild flowers for a museum or something." Margaret glanced at the picture again. "She came up here last year after the rain and stayed for four weeks. We knew where the flowers had come out, so we showed her where they were and I used to stay and watch."

"Did she let you use her paints?"

"She gave me an old box she said she didn't want any more. They were little tubes like toothpaste, but there aren't any left now."

"Your father would have got some more paints for you if you'd asked him, Margaret."

"Hm." Margaret's face clouded. "I haven't had a

birthday since then. He probably wouldn't have thought much of my pictures anyway."

"Didn't he ever see them?"

"I don't think so. We're always in bed by the time he's finished with the tourists."

Elizabeth held back a sigh. The tourists always gained more than their fair share of Mark's time, while his own children were growing up almost unnoticed.

"I hope you kept all your paintings, Margaret. I'd love to see them."

The girl bit her lip and considered for a moment. "You're just saying that."

"No I'm not. I'm really looking forward to seeing some more."

Margaret brightened. "They're in my room. Are you coming for dinner tonight?"

"Yes. How about bringing them out when the others have gone to bed? Then it'll be all nice and quiet and we can look at them together."

CHAPTER TWELVE

THAT ARRANGEMENT gave Margaret the excuse she needed to join the group at story time. Afterwards she carried a cardboard box into the living-room and pulled out the pictures she was willing to show. Elizabeth was impressed by her talent, but no special efforts were needed to convince Margaret that the praise was genuine. For the first time the girl was talking without reluctance or resentment. She named each flower, explaining which were hardy and which required heavy rainfall before they bloomed, and which she thought had a true colour likeness.

"I tried this one lots of times, but I couldn't get it right. It's pinker than that, but when I tried to get it pinker it didn't look blue enough."

"When you've had more practice at mixing colours you'll probably get it. I hope it rains again soon. I'd love to see all the wild flowers."

Margaret lost all her reticence, rummaging down to the bottom of the box for old and forgotten pencil drawings, scattering several pieces of paper over the floor. When she tidied up at last Elizabeth returned to her own quarters, glowing with satisfaction at the new turn of events. She must write to Jean at once and ask for more paints and a book on art. If a plane came in tomorrow the pilot could post the letter for her.

The days passed pleasantly, the isolated position of the ranch giving Elizabeth as much comfort and ease as she had hoped. Rufus was faithful to her alone, following wherever he was allowed and preventing any twinges of loneliness, and Charles was a congenial companion who often walked with them. Charles often seemed rather awkward and formal with other members of the staff, but he chatted readily with her and she enjoyed the hours they spent together. The only cloud over her happiness lay in her doubts about the children's honesty.

Normal high-spirited children could always be expected to play pranks, but without any signs of discomfort all five would solemnly assure her that they had nothing to do with the strange inhabitants she found in the drawer at school. She had trembled for several minutes after a grasshopper had leapt out at her, and after finding a cockroach and other species of beetles she had come to expect the worst, opening the drawer gingerly each time.

She said nothing to other people about her experiences, and whenever Annie or Olive enquired about the children's conduct she assured them that there were no problems at all.

"Doesn't sound like them. Must be saving it all up

for some special occasion," grumbled Annie. In an audible aside she added, "Though there's some as don't seem to recognise bad behaviour when they see it. Modern ideas and all that."

The regular pilot arrived earlier than usual one morning, bringing a mail bag and passengers on a day trip. He told Elizabeth that he had a letter for her, and as he handed it over he tried to steal a kiss. She had always tried to avoid him and escaped quickly, but she was still feeling ruffled when she entered the schookoom. She opened her drawer and thrust a heavy book inside without a glance, then faced her pupils for the usual little chat before starting work. When she opened the drawer again for her marking pen a peculiar smell arose.

"That's a stink bug," declared Brian.

"What do you mean? Some kind of smelly trick?"

"No, Miss Gaunt. A stink bug. Like a green beetle, only it stinks if you hurt it."

"You mean there must be a beetle in my drawer again."

"Yes. I'll get it for you." Brian moved one or two papers then lifted the book. "Aah! Look, Miss Gaunt. It's been squashed flat."

Elizabeth stared at the loathsome crushed insect. "Somebody must have put it inside. Now, who was it?"

"Not me, Miss Gaunt," they choroused.

"We wouldn't want anything to get hurt like that," said Pauline. She seemed close to tears over the death of the creature.

"I should hope not," answered Elizabeth sternly. "Take it away please, Brian."

She could sense the smouldering resentment in the group as Brian cleared the remains away. Far from enjoying a joke, they all seemed sorry for the unfortunate insect and piqued because she blamed them for the incident.

"I'm sorry if I snapped at you," she said. "I was feeling a bit cross about something else and that fright made it worse. Besides, I was sorry for the poor thing being killed like that."

Her last words cheered them all. "Some people kill things for nothing," said Brian. "Just because they don't like them. They should just put them outside, shouldn't they?"

There was a murmur of agreement, and with the resilience of children they resumed their schoolwork as though nothing had happened. At play time Elizabeth opened her letter and found the photographs she had taken in her first week. The colours were excellent and Jean and Bob had congratulated her on the results.

"Photographs!" exclaimed Carl as the children filed back into the room. "Did you get those this morning, Miss Gaunt?"

"Yes. Come and see the ones I took of you."

Someone had obviously trained them not to handle photographs. None of them attempted to pick one up, and when Pauline pointed a little too closely,

Julie gave her a warning nudge.

"You all look very smart on these," said Elizabeth, indicating the prints of the children on their first day at school. "My sister-in-law likes this one with the bikes, though, because you all look happier."

"I like every one," declared Pauline. She looked up at Elizabeth apprehensively. "People don't usually take our picture unless they're leaving."

"Don't worry, I'm not leaving," Elizabeth assured her. "I'll take some more soon."

"I wish they were black and white," said Margaret.

"Really! Why don't you like them coloured?"

"They show our red hair."

Brian and Julie nodded in agreement and Elizabeth stared at them in amazement. "But your hair is a beautiful colour."

"Most people don't think so."

"Of course they do. Some people like that colour so much they have their own dyed."

"Well, we've never met anyone that likes it. Everybody says it gives you a bad temper."

Elizabeth chuckled. "I know some people are always saying things like that. But if someone keeps saying you must have a bad temper, they're bound to end up making you cross. That has nothing to do with the colour of your hair."

"Patricia always said it had," declared Brian.

"And Nancy. She was one of the housemaids."

"And Mrs. Fenn hates it. She's always talking about us red-haired brats," added Carl.

"You shouldn't take any notice of things like that," protested Elizabeth weakly.

"It's all right for you," argued Margaret. "You haven't got red hair."

"No, I haven't." Elizabeth sighed, then continued, "But I used to have."

The five stared at her in astonishment, admiring the silver waves.

"Did you dye it?" asked Margaret at last.

"No, I had an accident. People often say that they nearly went white with shock. The accident gave me a bad shock, and afterwards my hair went this colour."

"I like it," said Pauline. "I wish mine looked like that."

"Well, it probably will when you're an old lady. You'll just have to be patient."

"Were you very ill?" asked Margaret.

"Yes I was, for a very long time."

Pauline leaned forward and gently stroked Elizabeth's arm with one finger. "Is that why your arms are different colours?"

"Pauline!" Margaret gave a gasp of dismay, but Elizabeth shook her head and smiled.

"Don't worry, Margaret. She isn't old enough to have learned how to be tactful." She looked down at the skin grafts and decided to tell the children about them." I lost a lot of skin, so the doctors had to put some more on. Some people get burnt so badly the doctors can't help them at all. That's why you must always be very, very careful with fire."

After school that day Elizabeth felt too restless to wander with only Rufus for company, so she decided to visit Rose. She had only been to the house once since the evening when she met Bill and Lesley, but Rose gave her no cause to feel guilty. "Hello," she said cheerfully. "You've given me the ideal excuse to drop everything and have a cup of tea. Or would you rather have a cool drink."

"No, I would prefer tea, thank you."

"Come on in, then. You can bring Rufus in if you like, but I expect he'll be quite happy sniffing around outside."

They exchanged small-tank until the tea brewed, then Elizabeth gave a shame faced smile. "I hate to admit it, but I came here to borrow something."

"Well, that's what friends are for, isn't it? What do you need? Some kind of gadget?"

"Steve mentioned his books about insects. I was hoping to borrow one."

"You'd better be careful or you'll end up with an armful," laughed Rose. "You been finding more in the school-room?"

"Have you heard about that?"

"The kids come and tell their Auntie Rose all kinds of things. Brian brought that spider down here to show Steve. It really was a whopper, wasn't it?"

"Did he tell you where it came from?"

"Your desk, apparently. He was very indignant that day. He said you'd accused him of putting it there."

"He seemed the most likely one at that time."

"Well, it's most odd. I mean, it's not the kind of prank they'd get up to. They'd be too concerned about the insect to treat it like that."

"I flattened something they called a stink bug today."

"Maybe you'd better change your table. Oh, there goes the baby. I'll be back in a minute."

The thin wails ended quickly as Rose changed the wet nappy and cradled the baby in her arms. She returned to the living-room and Elizabeth stared at the infant.

"She's grown," she said at last.

"Like the proverbial weed. Would you like another cup of tea?"

"Yes please. But I'll get it. Wouldn't you like one?"

Elizabeth was pleased to occupy herself with a job and was calm when she carried the cups back. Rose told her about the baby's increase in weight, then talked about the gossip she had heard on the radio.

"Can't have any secrets out here," she chuckled. "It's part of my job to listen in for telegrams. Nobody at the ranch has time for that sort of thing. And I send the weather. Oh, the weather! What's the time?"

She moved her arm to look at her watch and gave

another exclamation. "Time I got moving on that. Hold Barbara for me, would you?" She rose to her feet as she spoke and held the baby towards Elizabeth.

"Oh, I don't think…" Elizabeth cringed away.

"Don't worry, you won't have any trouble. All you have to do is sit there. I'll be finished in a tick."

Elizabeth opened her arms obediently and took the baby from her. Rose stood for a few seconds smiling down on them, then she patted the child gently and moved briskly away to record the meteorological details. Elizabeth sat rigidly at first, but as she looked into the large blue eyes staring up at her the stiffness faded away. She moved Barbara so that her head nestled more comfortably into the crook of her arm and began to talk softly to her. Six months ago she had been convinced that she would never be able to stand the close proximity of a baby again; it would be far too painful and bring back too many shattering memories. But Barbara was such a sweet little thing. Surely nobody could resist her not she or anybody else. Even the caustic Annie and the sullen Olive would melt under the charm of that steady gaze.

She did not notice Rose observing her from the doorway. By that time Barbara had a tight hold on her left thumb and she was holding the child with the aplomb that comes from practice. Soon afterwards Barbara began to whimper and Rose returned from the kitchen.

"Tea-time," she announced. "Her interior clock works well."

Elizabeth handed the baby into her arms and Rose hugged her fondly. "She's on a mixture of breast and bottle feeding. Would you like to give her the bottle when she's ready for it?"

Elizabeth scarcely hesitated. "Yes please."

"We won't be long. Help yourself to a magazine."

As she waited, Elizabeth wondered why she had agreed.

Supposing she broke down and caused a scene? But when the baby was nestling in her arms once more her alarm vanished. Rose watched her handling the infant — taking note of her skill, but saying nothing. The new govemess must have had a dramatic past, but it was still too early to expect her to speak about it.

CHAPTER THIRTEEN

" THE CHILDREN tell me you once had auburn hair," said Mark. "I hope they didn't embarrass you, asking awkward questions."

"Not at all," answered Elizabeth quickly. "We were having a discussion about hair, and I happened to tell them, that's all."

"They like that silver colour," Mark felt an urge to stroke it and hastily clasped his hands behind his back. "They've got good taste, I must say. I like it myself. When I first saw it I thought it was dyed."

"I quite like it myself now that I'm used to it." Elizabeth sought a way to switch the conversation. "Did Margaret show you that painting last night?"

"Yes. I was absolutely amazed. Did she really do that by herself?"

"Entirely by herself. She has plenty more to show you when you have the time."

Mark frowned. "There was plenty of time last night. Why didn't she show me then?"

Elizabeth hesitated. It was difficult to explain the situation without offending him. He loved the children in his own way and would not understand how they could feel unwanted. "She's a bit shy about them," she said finally. "Some evening when you have nothing else to do she'll bring them out. She's wary of wasting your time."

"Sometimes I'm certain the kids and I aren't on the same wavelength. You seem to get on with them much better than I do."

"We spend a lot of time together. That's bound to make a difference. And it's not unique. We often get complaints that children pay more attention to their teacher than to their parents."

"Seems I'll have to find more time somehow." Mark swept the blond streak back with his customary gesture and jerked his head in the direction of the main building. "I was just going over for a cup of tea. Coming?"

Olive glared coldly as they entered together, but Elizabeth paid no attention. Noreen was bubbling over with more than her usual goodwill, and explained that she was travelling to Alice Springs in the coach for a few days off.

"Course, it's not going to be all merry-making," she said. "I've to see the dentist amongst other things. D'you want me to bring anything back? Toothpaste, or lollies, or little intimate whatnots?"

"I would like some cartridge paper, please. Twenty-five sheets of the largest size."

Noreen fumbled for a list tucked in her brassiere. "There must be more exciting things you could do with. Think hard, because I won't be going again for ages and men aren't very good at shopping."

The commotion in the kitchen was worse than usual the next morning as they prepared for the coach's departure. Noreen assisted with gusto, breaking off every now and again for a joke and a hearty peal of laughter.

"For goodness' sake get out of here and let's have a bit of peace and quiet," said Annie.

"You'll miss me when I've gone. This place'll be like a tomb."

"Good luck to the tourists, that's all I can say. They won't get a minute's peace on the way in."

"Are you sure you can manage without me?" asked Noreen, as Mark appeared in the doorway.

"Fat lot of chance of stopping you now," he retorted. "Yes, we'll manage. Don't be cheeky to the dentist or you might come out with less teeth than you bargained for."

Noreen went out the back way to wave to the children, and all the tourists waved and grinned as George drove the coach past the kitchen. Obviously Noreen had provided entertainment already. Only Louise looked glum as the vehicle disappeared in a cloud of dust. Noreen brought the only light atmosphere into the kitchen, so a week without her would not be much fun.

The children were whispering together when Elizabeth entered the house and Brian was looking worried. He hesitated when she asked what was wrong, then muttered, "I've lost a scorpion."

"A scorpion!" Elizabeth could not conceal her

horror.

Brian nodded. "If it's in the house somewhere and Dad finds it, he'll go mad. He won't let me keep things like that in the house."

He was looking so guilty it was easy to guess the truth.

"I suppose you had it in the house," said Elizabeth.

"Yes. But it was only for one night. I couldn't find another place for it because it was going dark. I hid it under the bed."

"I wouldn't fancy keeping a scorpion under my bed."

"It was safe enough. At least, I thought it was. How was I to know it could chew a hole big enough to get out?" Brian scratched his head, torn between alarm and disappointment. "I wanted to show it to Steve. I'm sure it was pregnant."

"They have lots of babies and they carry them on their backs,"offered Pauline.

"Oh dear. So if you don't find it soon you might have a house full of scorpions." Elizabeth looked at her watch and came to a quick decision. "We've plenty of time yet before School of the Air. You can have fifteen minutes to look for it."

The children scattered to search the rooms, but came back empty-handed. Elizabeth peered fearfully into her drawer, a superstitious streak suggesting that it could be there, then they all tried to settle down for the start of the radio session.

"It's probably found a way out by now," said Margaret.

"Anyway, even if Dad does see it, he won't know you brought it in," said Carl. "Not if we don't tell him."

"As long as he doesn't ask," answered Brian morosely.

He spent his lunch hour hunting for the creature, then decided it was lost for ever and turned his attention to other matters. Elizabeth was thoughtful as she tidied up afterwards. Brian at least was not deceitful. He had given himself away immediately over his disobedience in keeping the scorpion inside the house.

Rufus was waiting to escort her to the cabin. She opened the bathroom door for him and watched in amusement as he sidled forward to investigate something that had attracted his attention.

"What have you seen now, Rufus? Oh, my goodness!" She grabbed the puppy and dragged him back as she caught sight of the creature in the corner. Its long pointed tail curled menacingly over its back, making sharp stabbing motions as it changed position. A wave of sickness swept over Elizabeth before she pulled herself together and hustled Rufus into the bedroom, closing the bathroom door behind her.

There was nobody near to help, but she had watched the children catching insects often enough, so she hurriedly tipped out an assortment of pencils, pens and paint brushes from a large jar she had salvaged from the rubbish heap. It took several moments to summon up her nerve to open the door again, and even then she hesitated. Rufus disobeyed orders and crept in, which gave her the impetus to act and seconds later the scorpion was imprisoned, fighting ineffectually against the heavy glass.

When she was satisfied that the creature could not escape, Elizabeth went in search of the children. They were all at the stables, talking to Steve, but they did not rush off as they used to when she approached.

"I've trapped a scorpion in my cabin, Brian," she said. "Would you get rid of it for me, please? I was scared to try slipping the paper under it."

"Is it a big one, Miss Gaunt?"

"I don't really know how big they're supposed to be. I've only seen pictures of them. It was certainly big enough to frighten me."

As usual, the other children refused to be left out of the action. They all jumped onto their bicycles and pedalled furiously up the hill, giving no regard to the heat.

"Well, that'll be a consolation prize for the one he's lost," said Steve. "I see you forgot your hat in the excitement. You'd better come into the shade."

Elizabeth followed him to the log under the tree and he rolled a cigarette leisurely. Their companionable silence was broken by a whoop of joy and the children rode back to the yard. Brian was clutching the large jar to his chest, his face red and shiny with pleasure.

"Miss Gaunt, it's the same one. It's the one I lost."

"Oh, it couldn't be, Brian."

"It is. Look how fat it is. It's pregnant, isn't it, Steve?"

The stableman took the jar from him and studied the angry creature inside. "It could be," he agreed cautiously. "Yes, it might very well be."

"I told you it was the same one, Miss Gaunt. I'd never seen one quite like it before."

"But my cabin's a long way from your house. It couldn't possibly have gone there."

"It probably went there because it knew you'd be kind," said Pauline. "Nobody else would have caught it. They'd have killed it."

Elizabeth smiled faintly, knowing that she would have killed it had her courage been stronger. It was the thought of the horrible squelch and the danger of missing it that had forced her to use a jar instead.

"I reckon it's the same one, too," declared Carl. "Are you going to keep it, Steve?"

"We'll keep it a while and see if you're right about it having babies. You know where to put the jar."

The five darted away towards Steve's house and he watched them disappear before turning to Elizabeth again.

"It's a funny thing about those insects you keep finding in your desk," he said. "And very strange that a similar scorpion should turn up in your cabin the very same day that Brian loses one." He took a long draw on his cigarette and watched the smoke as he exhaled. "Odd how it escaped, too. Didn't sound plausible when Brian said it had chewed its way out."

"It must be one of the children playing tricks. But I can't understand it. None of them seems to get any fun out of it."

Steve shook his head. "It's very strange. I wouldn't have been a bit surprised if it had been Patricia or one of the others, but I'm quite sure none of them wants to frighten you away. They're more settled and happy now than they've been for ages."

The raucous cawing of crows still awakened Elizabeth soon after dawn, so she was already partly dressed and reading a book when Olive knocked on her door the next day.

"You awake, Elizabeth?"

"Yes, come in. What's the matter?"

"Louise is sick so she can't come in today. You'll have to help out."

"Is she very bad?"

"Don't think so. Hurry up, we're running late."

Olive strode away and Elizabeth slipped her dress over her head, fuming at the other woman's attitude. She was quite willing to help anybody in a time of need, but it would have been pleasant if Olive had asked for assistance instead of taking her services for granted. As a gesture of rebellion she took longer than usual to comb her hair, checking carefully with a mirror to ensure that the scar was covered. No wonder Louise had looked so downcast when Noreen left. She must have been feeling unwell then.

"So here you are," was Annie's greeting. "Right old turn up for the book this is. What a time for Noreen to go away."

"Well, I can give you a hand for a while. What needs doing most?"

"Tables first," answered Olive.

Elizabeth set the tables while Olive busied herself slicing bread, mixing dried milk and filling dishes with marmalade.

"You need twenty-six cups and saucers," she instructed. "Put them on that side table, then fill the percolator up to the second mark."

When the dining-room was ready Elizabeth returned to the kitchen. Annie was stirring the porridge, watching Olive over her shoulder.

"What system are you going to use?" she demanded. "Let's get things straight now before that mob hits us."

"Depends on Elizabeth." Olive stopped work for a moment. "Do you want to wait on one of the tables yourself? If you don't think you can do it, you can stay in here and set the orders up on trays for me."

Elizabeth stared in confusion. "Wait on the tables?"

"You don't have to. I'll take the orders and carry them in. You can set them up ready for me."

"But I've got the school. I won't have time to stay

right through breakfast."

"You'll have to forget school today," snapped Annie. "We can't have tourists waiting an hour to get served."

Elizabeth's temper flared. "You're always fussing about the children's so-called lack of discipline. But now you say we ought to forget about school. Just because it suits you."

"The tourists are more important."

"Why are they? There are only twenty-five of them. A waitress in the city serves twice that number, or even more."

Olive drew herself up indignantly. "We don't keep the tourists waiting here like they do in other places. They get their meals straight off the stove."

"Well, this morning the service will have to be a little slower."

"I knew it would come to this," said Annie. "It's no use bringing a city teacher to the outback. They get such high-faluting ideas about themselves they can't face less glamorous work. I suppose you think it's beneath your dignity to wait on tables."

"Not at all. I shall be able to help at dinner."

Olive smiled coldly. "Mark will be back soon. He'll put you on breakfast and lunch, too."

"He most certainly will not."

"Want to bet?"

"Mark has more respect for his children's education than you two seem to have. I'll go and see him now. Where is he?"

146

"Putting fuel in the bus."

As Elizabeth headed for the back door, Annie tried to get in the last word. "I've always said those children shouldn't be here. They're a liability and only interfere with the running of this place."

Elizabeth opened the door, paused there and turned to face the other women again. "Annie, hasn't it occurred to you that if the children weren't here, I wouldn't be here either? In that case I wouldn't have been able to help at any time. Not now or at dinner." With that parting shot she made her exit, leaving Annie for once too flabber gasted to reply.

CHAPTER FOURTEEN

MARK WAS not at the fuel pump or inside the garage, so Elizabeth decided to try the house next. Brian was in the garden and he directed her to a veranda at the back of the building.

"I'm just getting dirt off," said Mark, rubbing his hands vigorously with an old rag. "I've been messing about in the engine. What's the problem?"

Elizabeth had simmered down since leaving the other women, but she was still determined to come straight to the point.

"Olive and Annie expect me to drop schoolwork today and help in the kitchen."

"Oh, yes. Louise has got flu or something," answered Mark. He examined his palms, then turned his hands over to inspect the nails. "Every body piles into help when need be."

Elizabeth took a deep breath. She must remain calm if she were to state her case clearly, but Mark spoke again before she had chosen her words.

"The children can manage. I told you they'd often done it before. They don't need you there for School of the Air, and Margaret can keep order afterwards."

"I thought you said the children came first with

you."

"Of course they do."

"Look, I don't want to be argumentative, but I don't think the priorities are right here." Mark looked up in surprise and she pressed on with her views. "Tourists are human, just like anybody else. If you explained that some of the staff were off sick they'd be quite willing to accept a few delays. After all, they're only here for two or three days. You'll have lots more tourists, but you won't have any more children."

There was a long pause. Mark studied the rag and Elizabeth bit her lip, wondering whether she could have said the same thing with more diplomacy. At last Mark looked up.

"You struck home with that one."

"I'm sorry. I shouldn't have said it."

"No, I'm glad you did. You obviously thought it, and I needed to be reminded." Mark looked at the rag again, then suddenly bundled it up and threw it into a corner. "I've been trying to hide myself in work, but that hasn't done the children any good. They're growing up, and I'm missing out. No wonder I don't seem to know the kids properly any more. I spend so much time fussing after tourists that the kids think they don't count. Margaret thinks I haven't even got time to look at her paintings."

"You could soon reassure them."

"You don't think it's too late?"

"Of course not."

Mark clenched his fists and opened them several times. "It's been a struggle here, but not in the last year or two. I think it just became a habit, spending so much time with the tourists. After all, I've got George to help with them now."

Elizabeth could think of nothing helpful to say so she remained silent. Mark strode along the veranda and back, smoothing his hair restlessly with one hand, then faced her again, legs wide apart, hands on hips.

"You know, I've often let the kitchen staff borrow the children's governess. I never gave serious thought as to how they'd feel about it. I had the vague idea that they might be pleased to have a day off, but thinking about it now I realise how dangerous that can be. The kids could easily get the feeling that they didn't count."

Elizabeth nodded and Mark clapped his hands together decisively. "Things are going to be different around here. If things go wrong in future, the tourists will just have to wait. The family comes first, no matter what."

Elizabeth smiled with relief and he grinned back at her. "The kitchen will manage perfectly well without you. I can make toast and wait on tables, and Rose will be able to help with the rooms and the washing-up later. Have you had your breakfast yet?"

"Not yet, but it won't take me long. I don't eat much in the mornings."

"I'd better go ahead of you and tell Annie that you

won't be there to help."

"I've already told her that."

Mark stared in astonishment, then threw his head back and roared with laughter. "You're a little firecracker, aren't you? Not nearly as meek as you look." He laughed again. "Gee, I wish I'd been there to see. Annie must have been speechless."

"She was."

"You must be the first one to achieve that," chuckled Mark. "Look, you give me a couple of minutes to get in the kitchen first. I want to hear her version before you arrive."

He went down the back steps and walked quickly away, still grinning at the image of the sour Annie Fenn being outfaced by the delicate young teacher. Elizabeth lingered on the veranda, wondering what kind of reception she would have next time she entered the kitchen. A slight noise caught her attention, and she turned to see Margaret in the doorway.

"Oh. Hello, Margaret."

"Hello, Miss Gaunt." The girl stayed where she was, gazing doubtfully at her teacher. "Did Dad mean what he said just now?" she asked at last.

"Yes, of course he did," replied Elizabeth, trying to think how the conversation had unfolded. How much had Margaret overheard?

"Did he really mean that we count more than the tourists?"

"Of course he did," Elizabeth repeated. "He

might not have said that to you, but that's what he thinks."

"Are you sure?"

"I'm positive." Elizabeth gave a confident smile. "I don't know how much you heard your father say, but he told me just now that the family comes first no matter what."

"I heard that," answered Margaret. "He was saying something about my paintings when I came out of the shower." She pointed to a window opening onto the veranda. "That's my room. I didn't think we'd have any school today because I knew Louise was ill."

"Well, you probably heard your father telling me he used to think you'd enjoy a day off. How do you feel about it? Do you wish we weren't having school today?"

Margaret pondered for a moment. "No, I like school now. It's much more fun with you. And it's going to be nicer than ever now that we know it's more important than tourists."

Annie was very polite to Elizabeth after that and seemed to have far more respect for her. She thanked her for the help she gave until Louise was better, and when Noreen returned everybody livened up. Annie even made a special cake.

"Wow, I'm an honoured guest," said Noreen.

"Well, come on then, sit down," ordered Annie. "Tell us the news. We're all waiting."

"Well now, let me see. I've been doing lots of

152

visiting." Noreen went on to tell them about people in Alice Springs, unknown to Elizabeth but interesting to hear about all the same. When George departed to drive his tourists to the gorge, Charles and Louise went back to their jobs but the others stayed to chat, Annie making pastry while she directed the conversation with pointed questions and remarks. She had covered the huge pie dish and was checking the oven when a timid knock came at the back door and Margaret's head appeared.

"Excuse me. Dad, there's a snake."

"A snake!" Mark went rigid and once again that strange expression appeared on his face, the look that Elizabeth had told herself she had imagined when she had mentioned snakes.

"A snake!" he repeated, gaining control of himself almost at once. "What kind? And where is it?"

"In the woodpile, Dad. Carl's keeping an eye on it. It's a King Brown."

"What do you mean, Carl's keeping an eye on it?"

"He's just watching to make sure it stays there, Dad. He's nowhere near it really."

Annie gave an exaggerated sigh, wiped her floury hands on her apron and bent down beside the gas stove. She straightened up again holding the small axe that she used to trim firewood for the cooking range.

"I'll fix it. I'm not scared of snakes. I've dealt with plenty in my lifetime."

"No, I'll take care of it." Mark rose to his feet suddenly and took the axe from her. "You get on with dinner, Annie. I'll look after this."

Noreen followed Mark, and almost against her will Elizabeth went too. Margaret walked along beside her, speaking more freely now that she was away from the forbidden territory of the kitchen.

"Brian went for Steve, Dad, and we told the girls to stay in the house."

"Who saw it?"

"Brian. He was looking for a long stick to make something with."

Elizabeth needed no prompting to stay at a safe distance, but Noreen went ahead to help Mark in moving the wood.

"You stay back, Noreen. I can manage perfectly well."

The Land Rover drove past the main building at that moment and roared towards them over the hard, dusty ground, cutting off any argument. Steve jumped out, closely shadowed by Bluey, and Brian climbed down from the other side. "Let Steve get it, won't you, Dad? He's got his snake stick."

Steve ordered his dog to sit, then collected a heavy sack and the snake stick from the back seat. "I'll take it right out beyond the range, Mark," he said. "It won't cause any trouble there."

Mark hesitated, then nodded his head reluctantly. "Okay, go ahead. But if you have any trouble catching it, I'm going to fix it once and for all."

Steve grinned and the two men went to the woodpile, carefully removing the assorted branches and bits of old timber. Elizabeth watched anxiously, wanting to flee and yet held there by some strange fascination. At last the men caught sight of the snake. Steve stretched his hand out for his equipment, moved one more piece of wood, then deftly trapped the reptile in the special tongs. Certain that it was secure, he turned around and held the snake out towards the women. It writhed endlessly, but Elizabeth could not resist a step forward.

"There you are, Elizabeth, a King Brown. Quite a heakhy specimen. Have you ever seen one before?"

ELizabeth gulped. "No, never. They're poisonous, aren't they?"

"Yeah," answered Steve casually. "You have to treat them with respect."

"I wish you'd treat this one that way and get it away from here," snapped Mark.

"Okay, okay. I know you can't stand them." Steve dropped his wriggling burden into the sack and closed the opening with a special cord fastener. "That's safe enough now."

The others waved him off, Mark's relief plainly visible, then they went back to the kitchen and resumed their gossip about Noreen's trip.

Mark kept his good intentions about spending more time with his family, joining them unexpectedly for dinner sometimes when Elizabeth was there. One afternoon he even accompanied them on a jaunt by horseback. Elizabeth was glad to see him, for although she had taken more lessons she had never dared to ride without Steve before.

The horse ambled along and Elizabeth made no attempt to hurry him. She was enjoying the peace and the view of the mountains never failed to enthral her. She thought how lucky she had been to see the advertisement in the paper. If things continued the way they were at present she would be quite satisfied to stay for ever.

Mark had glanced back several times to make sure she was coping well, and now he trotted to meet her, swinging his mount around and slowing to a walk beside her.

"Is William being lazy?"

"I like him to go slowly like this," answered Elizabeth. "If William speeded up I wouldn't have a chance to look at that lovely scenery."

"It is magnificent, isn't it?" Mark rode in silence for a moment, admiring the view. "Whenever I thought I'd made a mistake — about staying here I mean — I used to come out and look at that. It never failed. I always went back feeling better."He gave a short laugh as though the confidence had embarrassed him and pointed ahead. "There's a river bed where those trees are along there. We'll stop and bake some camp bread."

The children wandered away to play as they waited for the bread to bake beneath stones. Mark and Elizabeth settled in a shady spot under a tree and she leaned on her elbow to watch a large ant. She smiled as she thought how she would have been scared away only a few weeks ago.

"I'm glad you came," said Mark softly. "Things have been so different around here since you arrived."

He laid his hand lightly on her arm to convince her of his sincerity and Elizabeth sat up straight, jerking her arm away as though she had been stung.

"I'm sorry," he said. "You don't like to be touched, do you?"

"No." Elizabeth bit her lip, thinking she had been too terse. "I'm sorry. It's nothing personal, you understand."

"I think I understand. You were very badly hurt once, in more ways than one."

They were silent for several minutes after that. Elizabeth gradually unwound until she was leaning on her elbow again and Mark lay back with his hands clasped behind his head.

"Are you happy here?" he asked at last.

"Very happy," she answered. "I like the peace and the feeling that we're so far from anywhere the rest of the world can do what it likes." She tried to clear his serious expression with a joke. "Even with people like Annie Fenn around it's like heaven."

"Annie's going next week, thank goodness." He raised himself in his enthusiasm, supporting himself on his forearms. "You'll like Mrs. Chapman, Elizabeth. Everybody does, and the kids adore her."

He lay down again and stared into the branches above. "If you think it's like heaven now, you'll think it's absolute bliss when Mrs. Chapman takes over."

Another long silence followed, then Mark rolled over and gazed down at the sand." Elizabeth..."

"Yes?"

"I've heard that you spend a tremendous amount of time with Charles."

Elizabeth looked in surprise at his bowed head. "With Charles? Yes, as a matter of fact, I do. But I don't see what that has to do with anybody else. I suppose there's been nothing for people to talk about."

"Well, I don't want to poke my nose into your business. But I don't want you to get hurt again, either."

"I don't think there's any danger of that."

"There's always a possibility — if you get too fond of him." Mark began to trace endless circles in the sand with one finger. "I don't know quite how to put this, Elizabeth. I mean, I like Charles. He's a good worker and he's pleasant to everybody. But he came out here because he has a problem. He always kept himself to himself before you arrived." He finally twisted around to look at her. "What I'm trying to say is that he doesn't like women as such. He could never fall in love."

"I realised that ages ago," answered Elizabeth.

"You did?" Mark smiled with a mixture of

embarrassment and relief.

"Of course. That's why I don't mind being alone with him in the bush. I feel so safe with him."

"Oh." After a moment Mark chuckled bashfully. "I should have known you were wise to the ways of the world. But I hope you feel safe with me, Elizabeth. I don't want you to feel nervous in my company."

"I haven't been nervous up to now, anyway."

"I'm glad to hear it. I hope nothing happens to upset the peace now. I wouldn't like to lose you, and I know the children would miss you badly." Mark turned onto his back again and stretched slowly. "You know, I should have done this kind of thing more often. Left George in charge and come out with the kids."

CHAPTER FIFTEEN

ANNIE LEFT at the end of the following week after a short evening get-together. The gathering could hardly be called a party, for nobody could honestly say they would miss the caustic cook and they did not want to extend the occasion any longer than necessary. Noreen took over the cooking duties for a few days until Mrs. Chapman arrived to fill her old position, and a happy-go-lucky atmosphere prevailed.

The children had been excited ever since they heard that Mrs. Chapman was about to return and they talked of little else. Mrs. Chapman let them eat in the kitchen. Mrs. Chapman made biscuits like rabbits and teddy bears. Mrs. Chapman made paste for them on the stove. Obviously she had been a mother figure for the children and they had missed her sadly.

Rose carried the baby to the ranch one afternoon, and Louise immediately offered to nurse her while everybody talked.

"You'll have to take turns," laughed Rose. "Otherwise I'll be accused of favouritism." She turned to Mark. "I was talking to Lesley on the radio this afternoon. She wanted me to remind you about their welcome back party for Mrs Chapman."

"Oh, yes. Monday. I told the agent in town to make sure he didn't send any tourists out that day. We're going to close the shop for once."

"It'll be great fun," said Louise. "I've been to one of their parties and it was fantastic. You'll be able to meet more people, Elizabeth. Everybody will come from miles around."

Mrs. Chapman's return and the prospect of a party at the homestead, noted for its celebrations, was the sole basis of conversation until the weekend. Elizabeth found herself joining in the children's excitement and lingered near the buildings on Saturday morning. When the children shouted that a cloud of dust had appeared along the road, everybody rushed to see if the cook was arriving.

A pale blue battered car towing a cream caravan pulled up beside the kitchen door and the children ran towards it, shouting a welcome. Mrs. Chapman was a plump, round-faced woman, much younger than Elizabeth had imagined. She had been told that the regular cook was a widow and she had pictured an elderly, comfortable person who treated Mark's family like grandchildren. However, when she had hugged each of the children and made her way through to meet Mark and the staff, Elizabeth saw a woman with no sign of grey hairs, her only wrinkles caused by years of living in a hot, dry climate. She must only be in her forties, Elizabeth decided, as she watched the new arrival give Mark a friendly kiss.

"Hello, Mrs. Chapman. Good to see you," he said. "How was the trip?"

"Good, thanks. I told you I was going to take it in easy stages, didn't I?"

"Couldn't do otherwise with all the calls you were going to make on the way," he laughed. "Come and meet our new teacher."

Despite the turmoil of her arrival, the endless gossip and the children trailing in and out of the kitchen, the tourists were well looked after and the meals were ready on time. Mrs. Chapman had been told to relax the first day, but she could not resist taking part in the work and soon had an apron on. Only Olive protested about the children's visits to the kitchen, comparing the current confusion with the orderly routine of the past weeks.

Mrs. Chapman's happy beam faded. "Those children live here, remember," she snapped. "This is their home. They're not casual employees who'll move on when they get a mind to."

Olive made no response but she looked suitably chastened, and Mrs. Chapman resumed her description of a weekend visit to friends "up the track".

Elizabeth had taken an instant liking to the cook and easily understood why she was so welcome. Seeing Noreen alone in the laundry she stopped to chat with her.

"Noreen, why does everybody call Mrs. Chapman

by her full name? Nobody called Annie Mrs. Fenn, and Mark refuses to be called Mr. Hampton."

Noreen folded two more pillow slips, her lips pursed in thought. "I dunno. She's *always* been Mrs. Chapman. Perhaps because of the children. Why?"

"Well, don't tell her — but I was expecting somebody quite elderly."

"Hah! That's a good one," chortled Noreen. "Don't worry about telling her that. She's got a real sense of humour. She might even take it as a compliment."

Elizabeth had given a great deal of thought to the prospect of going to the party, but she was sorry to be asked a direct question about it at dinner when so many people were present. She had hoped to discuss the subject privately.

"What are you going to wear tomorrow, Elizabeth?" asked Louise gaily.

"Oh." Elizabeth saw everybody look at her and began to blush, but she decided not to dodge the issue. "As a matter of fact, I shan't be going after all."

"Not going!" gasped Louise.

"No. I'm sorry, Mrs. Chapman. I don't want to offend you or anything, but I'd rather not go."

"That's all right, my dear. Takes more than that to offend me."

"Why aren't you going?" asked Olive bluntly.

"Well, for one thing I don't drink." Elizabeth could imagine the trouble she would have, trying to prevent well-meaning people from adding alcohol to her fruit juice. "And for another thing, it's so far away. I won't be able to come back when I feel tired."

"I'll drive you back any time you like," offered Charles. "I'm taking my car."

"No, thank you. I'd rather not go." She looked around to make sure all the children had gone out and added, "Besides, the children will be here."

"They're not nervous," said Mark. "And they can call us on the radio if they want anything."

"I've already told them I'll be here," answered Elizabeth.

"I see."

To her relief the topic was dropped, but when she left the kitchen Mark came after her.

"Elizabeth, wait a minute." He put out his hand to detain her, but snatched it back, remembering how she had reacted the last time he touched her. "Elizabeth," he said again. "It's not because of the children that you decided not to go, is it?"

"No. I really would be happier here with them than at any party."

"The kids can go with us, you know. Bill and Lesley have lots of beds and they've slept there before. But the kids decided they'd rather stay here."

"That makes six of us then. Don't worry, Mark. I'm not trying to be noble or anything like that. I know I wouldn't enjoy myself and I'd prefer to be here."

Mark nodded." All right. I won't try to push you into it. Not that I could, I suppose. Even Annie Fenn couldn't browbeat you into anything."

Elizabeth felt no regrets as she watched the others making final preparations to depart the next day. Noreen looked smarter than ever before in a neat green and white cotton dress that managed to disguise her ample proportions. Louise was wearing a simple white dress that showed her dark hair off to advantage, while Olive emerged in a sophisticated royal blue garment that fitted perfectly. Her hair was swept up in a complicated arrangement on the crown of her head, and diamante earrings glistened in her ears. Elizabeth wondered when Olive had last found an opportunity to wear such an outfit, and what kind of life she had led before she came to the outback. Mark interrupted her thoughts. He had discarded the usual riding boots for ordinary shoes, but otherwise he was casually dressed.

"Are you sure you'll be all right, Elizabeth?"

"Of course. I'm going to enjoy myself sorting out the books — knowing that nobody can disturb me. It will be nice for the children to see a light in the lounge, too."

"It was lights I wanted to talk about. You remember I told you this morning I'd switch the generator off before we left?"

"I hope you haven't changed your mind. I'd be scared to death if anything went wrong with it while you were away."

"It's not likely to, but there's always a chance, I suppose, with that old thing." He held out a battery lamp with a fluorescent strip. "Mrs. Chapman has lent this so that you won't have to worry about spilling oil or anything."

"Thank you," said Elizabeth, wondering what he had told Mrs. Chapman. She knew he had asked for the lamp so that she could have light without using fire. What a pity he had neglected his own children so much when he was capable of such deep thought for comparative strangers.

At last everybody was ready and the cars were driven off. The children waved furiously, then they went back to their games in the bungalow until it was time for dinner. The little ones went to bed without fuss after a story, then Brian set to work on his latest model and Margaret curled up in a chair with a book. She enjoyed reading now that she had a choice of easy books and more confidence in her ability.

Elizabeth walked slowly back towards the main building and stopped about half way. She thought it had been peaceful here before, but she had never known such quietness as this. For the first time she was out here at night alone. The generator had been stopped and no voices disturbed her solitude. The only sounds to break that stillness were the shrill whim of countless cicadas and the repeated call of some far-off bird. An owl, perhaps? She turned to look at the sandhills and gasped with pleasure at the sight of the full moon rising majestically behind the dunes. It mounted steadily into the sky and hung there like a golden ball, casting a pale glow over the countryside.

"That's beautiful," breathed Elizabeth. Large moths and other insects had been drawn to her lamp and beat against the glass, but she disregarded them. She did not even mind when they fluttered against her hand. This was the closest she had been to serenity for many a long day. When she finally moved on she was smiling at her former timidity. She had been almost too scared to step out of doors after dark during her first weeks at the ranch, and then she had missed the beauty of the night sky by keeping her eyes fixed on the ground.

The noise of an engine was the first unexpected sound to disturb Elizabeth's peace. She looked up from her book, then glanced at her watch. Half past twelve, near enough. She hadn't realised how time was passing, but surely it was still too early to expect anybody back from the party. It must be a traveller looking for accommodation. She swung her legs down from the settee and tided her hair with one hand as she fumbled for her shoes. The vehicle stopped at the back of the building and the headlights were switched off. Elizabeth had stepped towards the door when a familiar voice called out, "It's only me, Elizabeth. Mark."

"Oh." She was hovering uncertainly in the centre of the room when he entered.

"I hope I didn't give you a scare."

"No, of course not. I thought it must be a tourist. You're early."

"Yes." Mark looked around, noting the open book on the small circular table and the newly arranged shelves on the far wall. "You've been busy, I see."

"Yes. I've been intending to go through those books since I first arrived."

"I had a bit of a sort out in my place the other day. The kids probably told you."

"Yes. Brian was very pleased with the bits and pieces you gave him."

They stood facing each other, both feeling awkward, then Elizabeth edged back towards the settee. "Is there anything the matter?"

Mark shook his head. "No, nothing's wrong. I just wasn't in the right mood for parties, and everybody else was having a good time so I came back alone." He followed her a little way across the lounge, then stopped again and thrust his hands into his trouser pockets. "Am I disturbing you? I'll go across to the house if you'd rather be alone — or if you want to go to your cabin."

"No, stay here by all means. I hadn't realised how late it was until I heard your car."

"Thank you." Mark sat at the opposite end of the long seat, staring into the empty fireplace, and Elizabeth waited for him to speak. Obviously he had something on his mind.

At last he turned slightly towards her, wedging his spine comfortably in the corner angle and resting his elbow on the back of the settee. "I felt like thinking tonight," he told her. "It was too noisy for that at the party so I didn't stay long. I've been two and a half hours on the road."

"It's a lovely night," said Elizabeth. "I stood outside for a long time."

"Yes. I must have been stopped a good hour. If not more." He looked away from her again. "It's a long time since I dared to stop and think. I'd been packing more and more into my days to make sure I hadn't the time for it. I didn't dare think about the past. But somehow, lately, it seemed too cowardly. I should have faced up to it before."

Elizabeth said nothing. Mark apparently felt a need to talk and she did not want to distract him.

"Do you know I've tried not to think about my wife for nearly six years," he burst out suddenly. "Wouldn't think of her because it upset me. That's not the way to behave, is it? Nearly six years and I've hardly looked at her photograph in all that time. The kids don't even know what she looked like. Their own mother!"

Elizabeth wished she had not become involved in this. Her own problems had caused anguish, but her experiences did not qualify her to help Mark through this troubled patch.

"Do you think it's right to bring five children up knowing nothing about their mother?" he demanded.

"Well…" faltered Elizabeth.

"It's not. You needn't try to spare me." Mark

sighed. "For the past week I've been trying to pluck up enough courage to talk to them about her. We've been talking more easily just lately, me and the kids, but I just couldn't get started. How do you introduce a subject like that after all this time?"

It did not sound like a direct question so Elizabeth made no attempt to answer it. Several moments passed before he glanced at her again.

"She had auburn hair."

"That would be a good starting point," suggested Elizabeth. "We had a discussion about hair quite recently."

"Mm." Mark was staring at the stone fireplace once more. "The past is past, isn't it? Life goes on. It has to. Where would we be if nobody ever tried to make a fresh start?"

After a short pause Elizabeth answered. "Sometimes the fresh start isn't as difficult as it would appear to be. It's the effort of actually making a move towards it that's the worst."

"You would know plenty about that, I dare say."

"I certainly branched out in a different direction. It seems to have done me good. More good than I had hoped."

"Sounds as though you're trying to urge me on." Mark forced a smile. "I'm thinking of taking an even bigger step than yours, though."

"Oh."

"I'm thinking about marriage."

"Oh," said Elizabeth again. So Olive's outfit and

special grooming had had the desired effect. It had prodded Mark into action at last.

"It doesn't sound as though you approve."

"Whether I approve or not has nothing to do with it," she answered lightly. "Actually I was taken by surprise. When you mentioned big changes I thought you had considered moving away from here."

"Do you honestly think that would be a good idea?"

"No," she replied quickly. "I couldn't imagine you settling in any other place. You'd always regret it."

"You're right there. That's one point I am definite about. I belong here. I made my mind up about that long ago."

"You haven't really got a problem, have you?" said Elizabeth after another long silence. "You feel a little guilty for some reason. But you've definitely made up your mind about getting married."

"There are lots of problems. The past still has to be reckoned with." Mark sighed again and ran his fingers through his hair. "I should tell the children about their real mother before I start to do anything about providing them with a new one, shouldn't I?"

"Yes, I think so." Elizabeth could not bring herself to say more or pretend any enthusiasm. Olive was hardly an ideal choice so far as the children were concerned and she pitied them. Before much time had passed they would probably be sent away to school after all. Olive had too little patience to deal with five children, especially a ready-made family from a previous marriage. One thing seemed certain. Her own position as teacher would not last much longer. She and Olive got on so poorly with each other there could be no question of her staying.

CHAPTER SIXTEEN

THE CROWS disturbed Elizabeth as usual the next morning, but she was tired after her late night and slipped back into sleep for two more hours. The kitchen was deserted and she saw nobody on her way to the bungalow, but the children were wide awake, clustered around a cardboard box on the veranda.

"Miss Gaunt, come and see what Uncle Bill sent." Pauline was excited but she remembered to keep her voice low. Obviously their father was still asleep.

"It's the first one I've ever seen," said Brian. "They're very rare."

Elizabeth looked over their shoulders and shuddered at the sight of the thin wriggling creature in Carl's hands. "Is that a snake?"

"No, Miss Gaunt. It's a legless lizard," answered Brian. "Do you want to hold it?"

"Yes, go on," urged Carl, holding it towards her.

"They don't bite," said Margaret. "Go on, Miss Gaunt, hold it."

Elizabeth succumbed to their pleas and Carl laid the reptile in her hand. It jerked nervously, then wound its long tapering tail around her wrist.

"It likes you," said Pauline. "Isn't it pretty?"

"Yes," answered Elizabeth dubiously. Contrary to her expectations the lizard felt warm against her skin. She had read enough to know that reptiles were not slimy, but she thought it would have been cold.

"Do you think Dad will let us keep it?" asked Brian anxiously.

"You'll help us to persuade him, won't you?" asked Margaret. "You know it's a nice friendly thing, and he'll take more notice of you."

"Don't you think...?" began Elizabeth, but approaching footsteps interrupted her question. Mark appeared at the interior door, smoothing his hair with one hand.

"Good morning. I thought you'd sleep in today."

"I slept longer than usual, but I set the alarm to make sure I wouldn't be late."

"I might have guessed you'd do that." Mark stepped towards them, but as Elizabeth turned he stopped short. "Elizabeth! What are you doing with that thing?"

"It's not a snake," she told him. "It's a legless lizard."

"Where did you find it?"

"It came from Bill, apparently."

"Well, he knows what he's talking about," said Mark in relief.

"Can we keep it, please Dad?" asked Brian.

"I suppose Steve brought it back."

"Yes, Dad. We went to see him when he was doing the six o'clock weather. We can keep it, can't we?"

Mark looked at the lizard that was still coiled around Elizabeth's wrist, and wiped his brow. "If Miss Gaunt can stand it, I suppose I can. But get it out of this house and don't expect me to have anything to do with it."

"Gee, thanks Dad. Steve's going to help me to make a proper place for it. And it'll hibernate soon." Brian took hold of the creature gently and the others followed him down the steps.

Mark watched them go with a sigh. "I can't bear the sight of anything that's even remotely like a snake. How could you bring yourself to actually hold it?"

"Well, they were so thrilled about it, and they persuaded me."

"Sometimes I think you'd do anything for those kids. I wish…" Mark broke off suddenly and began to walk away. "I'd better let you get on with your work," he muttered over his shoulder.

Everybody appeared for lunch except Olive, and although there were a few groans about late nights and headaches they all seemed to be in good spirits. They talked about the party and the latest gossip, and Louise described the fancy savoury dishes that she had enjoyed so much. When Elizabeth left the table Noreen ushered her to one side.

"Watch how you go with Olive," she murmured. "You've heard about bears and bad heads."

"You mean she's got a hangover."

"You might say so. Just steer clear, that's all."

Dropping into the kitchen for a cup of tea had become a regular routine for Elizabeth after school. She went across that afternoon as usual, smiling at a joke the children had told her. Mrs. Chapman was mixing a pudding and Olive was sitting alone at the table, staring into a half-filled teacup.

"Hello, Olive. Did you have a good time last night?"

Olive looked up and scowled. "What do you think?"

"Oh." Elizabeth had forgotten Noreen's warning. "I won't disturb you," she said belatedly. "I suppose you don't feel like talking."

"But I do feel like talking." Olive stood up and moved around the table to face Elizabeth. "You've got a nerve, asking me if I had a good time."

"Whatever do you mean?"

"You know. Don't try playing the innocent."

"I don't know what you're talking about. Has somebody upset you?" Elizabeth backed away, but the other woman came after her.

"Don't know what I'm talking about? And you the one that planned it all?"

"Planned what?"

"All that business about staying here, so that you and Mark could have the place to yourselves for a cosy little get-together."

"You've got it all wrong," protested Elizabeth.

Olive laughed scornfully. "Got it wrong indeed!

Are you going to tell me he didn't come back here last night? Why else would he leave the party?"

"He didn't come back till very late."

"Don't try to kid me you didn't see him."

"No, but…"

"You waited for him. You, who never goes to bed late. You knew he would come. So you waited."

"You seem to think I have designs on him."

"Well, haven't you?" demanded Olive. "Why else have you stayed here? You, who's scared of geckoes. You'll put up with spiders, scorpions and anything to get what you want."

"Scorpions!" breathed Elizabeth. Suddenly everything fitted into place. Olive tidied up the bungalow every day.

The answer to those inexplicable pranks became clear and her anger flared. "You can't scare me away with insects and things, Olive. That was a childish thing to do — putting spiders in the drawer. As if that would make me pack up and leave."

Now Olive backed away. "I don't know what you're talking about."

"Yes, you do. It was a stupid mistake to put that scorpion in my cabin. Even Steve guessed how it came to be there."

"You're just making silly accusations to try and change the subject."

"There's nothing more silly than your accusation. I'm not interested in Mark."

"Yes you are. I've watched you. And I watched

you with the baby when Rose was here the other day. You want a baby of your own." Elizabeth stepped back, pale with horror and Olive pressed her attack. "Mark's not been the same since you arrived and made eyes at him. He doesn't even come for barbecues any more. He goes over there and has dinner with you and the kids. You've been spoiling those kids just to get round him. Don't you try to deny it. Those kids have been used as an excuse every time you two want to get together."

Elizabeth drew herself up. "So far as I am concerned, I don't want to get together with anybody."

"You're just saying that. What about last night?"

"I assure you I mean every word. I have no intention of getting involved with any man ever again. Not Mark or anybody else."

"Why?"

"Never mind why. Just accept that." Elizabeth sighed heavily. "Look, it's ridiculous, arguing like this. You'll ruin your whole life if you let jealousy take over. I'm not trying to win Mark away from you and neither is anybody else. In fact, I think things are just beginning to go nicely your way."

"How do you mean?" Olive's eyes flickered with hope.

"Well, you know Mark left the party last night. But it wasn't to come back here. He was trying to decide whether or not it would be right for him to marry again."

"And he decided he would. About time he got around to that," declared Olive.

The door to the dining-room was suddenly flung open and it crashed against the corner of a serving table. Mark stood in the opening, breathing heavily, hands on hips, his face flushed.

"If you've quite finished discussing my future, perhaps I can get a word in," he snapped.

"Oh, I'm sorry. Did you hear your name mentioned?" Olive's voice had resumed the honeyed tones she kept for him.

"I heard every word of that ridiculous argument." Mark waved his right hand angrily. "You seem to forget that wall isn't solid. There's an old serving hatch there."

"I'm sorry, but we lost our tempers. I suppose we were shouting a bit."

"Well, now it's my turn. And to save any further bother I'll tell you straight — I have no intention of marrying you, Olive, and never had. How you came to imagine such a thing I have no idea."

"Mark!"

"I gave you no reason to believe that I was interested in marriage."

"Mark, it's understood all around here. Don't tell me you've been leading me on."

"I haven't been leading anybody on, and I fail to see how such a thing could be understood."

"But it is, Mark." Olive caught hold of his hand and gazed at him pleadingly. "You'll have to marry

179

me, Mark. Everybody expects it."

Mark dragged his hand away. "I've told you. I have no intention of marrying you. Any understanding as you call it is all in your own imagination."

Olive glared at him. "You can't brush me off as easily as that."

"What will you do? Put scorpions in my room?"

"You heard that story, too, did you?"

"I told you, I heard everything." Mark turned to Elizabeth. "Why didn't you tell me if things like that were going on? I said let me know if anybody tried to make things unpleasant for you."

Elizabeth spread her hands helplessly. "I thought it was meant as a joke."

"Those kind of jokes are not funny to anybody. Olive, you'll pack your bags and move out of here tomorrow. There'll be two planes in the afternoon. Pick which one you want."

"You can't throw me out just like that."

"You can take two weeks' pay in lieu of notice."

Olive stamped forward and glared at Mark, her cheeks glowing angrily. "It's going to take more than two weeks' pay to get rid of me. I've been wasting months here while you lead me on."

"Any leading on was all in your imagination. If you don't want the pay, go without it and then sue."

"I'll do better than that," stormed Olive. "I'll sell that map you lost. Even if you're not willing to pay well for it, other people will be."

180

Mark shook his head in bewilderment. "Now what are you talking about?"

"That map that shows where the gold reef is." Olive pointed her finger at him as he tried to respond. "Don't pretend you don't know what I'm talking about. I know you turned the whole house upside down looking for it last week."

"This is nonsense," protested Mark.

"Nonsense, is it? I'll show you whether I really have it or not." Olive flounced out through the dining-room and Elizabeth sidled towards the back door.

"Where do you think you're going?" demanded Mark.

"Well, I really don't think this has anything to do with me. I'll let you finish off in private. I should have gone before."

"Huh!" Mark's scorn stopped her in her tracks. "So you don't think this has anything to do with you! Not after telling Olive she had a free run in the marriage stakes? And marriage to me at that."

"I'm sorry. I was all het up. I said more than I should."

Mark walked slowly towards her, then turned sharply and strode away. He was rubbing the back of his head with one hand and muttering furiously under his breath.

"I'm sorry," said Elizabeth again.

He did not appear to have heard her, but he swung around as Olive rushed into the kitchen again.

"Here," she shouted, waving a tattered piece of paper at him. "Now say you know nothing about it."

"Let me see."

"Oh no you don't." Olive pulled the paper out of his reach. "You can't catch me as easily as that. I'm keeping this till you pay me what it's worth."

"I can't even see what it is."

"It's the map, I tell you. The map of the gold reef."

"Rubbish."

"Here, let me see that," said Mrs. Chapman suddenly. Everybody turned and stared. She had been continuing her work so quietly and unobtrusively they had forgotten her presence.

"It's a map," said Olive, recovering some of her former belligerence.

"So you said." Mrs. Chapman strained to see it from across the room. "It looks familiar. Does it include the sand-hills by any chance?"

"Yes. Why?"

Mrs. Chapman burst into laughter." That's not worth a bean, my dear. Margaret made it last winter."

"You're lying. It's old."

Mrs. Chapman shook her head and laughed again. "We put it in the oven to make it yellow. Somebody told the kids about Lassiter's Reef and they were playing at treasure hunts."

Mark gave a sardonic smile. "Looks as though you've played your last card, Olive. Tell us which plane you'll take and I'll get somebody to drive you to the airstrip tomorrow."

"Ugh!" Olive threw the map aside and Elizabeth watched it floating to the floor as the woman stalked away. She picked it up and was admiring the detail in the drawings', thinking how much effort Margaret put into projects that interested her, when she became aware that Mark was standing beside her.

"Elizabeth, whatever made you think that I'd be likely to marry a woman like that?"

"Well…" Elizabeth flushed. "I suppose I took it for granted."

"As she did. But why?"

"I suppose because I couldn't think of anybody else. And you said you were thinking of getting married."

"Not immediately, and certainly not to anybody like that. When I choose a wife it's going to be somebody who loves children. I said I was going to give them a new mother, remember? Can you imagine Olive as a mother? Surely you credit me with more —" Mark waved his hands in frustration, lost for suitable words. "Surely you have a better opinion of me than that," he finished.

Elizabeth bit her lip, staring at the paper in her hand and wondering what to say. When she looked up again he had turned away and she followed the direction of his gaze. Mrs. Chapman was still behind her workbench, imperturbably rubbing fat into flour. Mrs. Chapman! of course! She was about Mark's

183

age. She was a widow and she loved children. More important, the children loved her. Elizabeth frowned at her own stupidity. How could she have failed to think of Mrs. Chapman last night when Mark talked of his plans? Her tactless remarks this afternoon must have embarrassed both of them, especially as Mark was not ready to go ahead with those plans yet.

CHAPTER SEVENTEEN

ELIZABETH WEPT when she reached her cabin. After the tears were spent her next thought was to leave the ranch as soon as possible, but she discarded that idea when she had calmed down. The children would suffer if she walked out on them, and Mark would have problems enough with one member of staff short already.

She waited for a quiet moment to apologise to Mrs. Chapman. The cook received her as serenely as ever, and interrupted before she had stumbled far into her explanation.

"Look, my dear, no need to worry about having your row in front of me. The places I've been in, I'm used to ups and downs. Worked a season at a sheep station during shearing one year, so any kind of language would go right over my head."

"I said things I had no right to say." Elizabeth was close to tears again.

"Strikes me you were very reticent considering the things she'd done to you. And she said some very nasty things about you, too."

"I can't remember what was said now. I must have lost control of myself."

185

"All the better if it is forgotten. Don't you worry, my dear. If it's any consolation, you didn't use a single bad word."

Elizabeth wished the children were still eating their meals at the bungalow so that she would not have to face everybody, but the staff greeted her as though nothing had happened. The conversation naturally evolved around Olive and her imminent departure, but Elizabeth's part in the affair was not mentioned. Apparently the quarrel had been passed off as an eruption between Mark and Olive alone.

Mark still had his meals in the dining-room with the tourists, so Elizabeth managed to evade him for two days. However, on the third afternoon he kept watch for her leaving the house and called her back.

"Are you trying to avoid me?" he asked.

Elizabeth blushed. "Well, I suppose I am."

"Why? What have I done to deserve that kind of treatment?"

"I was too embarrassed. I mean, after what I did the other afternoon..."

Mark grinned down at her. "Look, forget it. I might have sounded annoyed. I was annoyed — then. But there's no need to keep on about it. I was just as stupid as the rest of you."

"I'll never forgive myself for the things I said. And the things I assumed..."

"Look, I said forget it. When you get right down to things, it was my fault. I must need my head examined. Fancy me thinking that Olive went to the barbecues because she liked the trip!" Mark gave a snort of self-derision. "Noreen didn't mince matters when she told me off."

Elizabeth smiled at the thought of Noreen putting him in his place. "She must have been very explicit."

"You bet your life she was. Still, as she pointed out, Olive must have had her doubts about the campaign. She wouldn't have kept that map as insurance, otherwise, would she?" Mark threw his head back and laughed aloud. "Poor Olive. She must have thought I was worth a mint. Imagine it — making so much money out of tourists I couldn't be bothered to dig the gold out of a mine!"

Affairs at the ranch settled down to an unruffled routine again and Elizabeth felt completely at ease. The weather was cooler now, enabling her to go out at any time of day without worrying about the temperature, and she dropped in to chat to Rose more readily than she had at first. The baby was growing stronger and Elizabeth no longer had qualms about nursing her.

The May holidays approached almost unheeded. Elizabeth was quite prepared to stay at the ranch and help the others, but Mark insisted that she went away to Adelaide.

"You need a rest from the kids. And I want your brother to see how fit you are now."

He made all the bookings as if to make sure she would go, and sent her by air so that she would have longer with Bob and Jean. She thoroughly enjoyed telling them all about her new life, but she soon began to miss her friends at the ranch and was pleased to return after two weeks.

The children ran to meet her at the airstrip, pushing each other aside in their efforts to hug her first. Mark waited in the background until the excitement died down a little, then stepped forward and held out his hand.

"Welcome back. Did you have a good trip?"

"Very good, thank you," answered Elizabeth, shaking hands with enthusiasm. "I've had a lovely time."

"I'm glad you came back."

"You didn't really think I wouldn't, did you?"

"Not really. But you never know when those city people get onto you." He collected her luggage from the pilot and they followed the children back to the car. "How does it feel to be out here again?" he asked.

"Marvellous. It's like coming home."

"That's all I wanted to hear. That really makes you one of us." Mark looked around to ensure they were out of earshot. "How did you get on with the traffic and the crowds in Adelaide? Did it worry you?"

"I was a bit nervous at first, but nothing like I was before."

"That's good." Mark grinned happily. "The Centre seems to have worked a cure. I hope your family was impressed."

A new girl had joined the staff during Elizabeth's absence. She joined the group who had assembled in the kitchen to welcome Elizabeth, and Noreen introduced her as Margaret Swinson.

"We call her Meg," she said. "So's we don't get mixed up with the other scallywag called Margaret."

"She plays a guitar," said Brian. "We've been learning some new songs."

"Good. It sounds as though you've been having fun while I've been away."

The taste of city life enabled Elizabeth to appreciate the peace of the ranch even more than before and she stood outside for several minutes before going to bed, looking at the stars.

Next day the weather seemed close and a veil of cloud obscured the sky.

"Building up for rain," said Noreen, stopping beside her as she stared upwards. "We thought we'd missed out when it cleared yesterday, but Mark reckons we'll get some now."

"It hasn't rained once since I came here."

"No, it's needed badly."

The clouds gathered for three days, anxiously watched by everybody. At last the storm broke and they were all awakened in the early hours of the morning by echoing booms of thunder and heavy drumming of rain on corrugated iron roofs. The rain persisted and at seven o'clock the children ran across to Elizabeth's cabin.

"Miss Gaunt, are you awake?"

"Yes, I'm up. Come in."

"We can't come in, we're sopping wet."

Elizabeth opened the door and found the five youngsters in a group outside, grinning happily as the rain streamed from their cotton clothes. None of them wore shoes and their legs were coated with red mud.

"Dad says no school today," announced Carl.

"We're going to the ranges to show you the waterfalls," said Pauline.

"If we have another long drought you might never see them again," Margaret informed her.

"Oh. Well, in that case we'd better take advantage of the weather, hadn't we?"

The mountains looked black from a distance, the colour changing to various shades of grey and purple as the Land Rover drew closer. The sun-baked earth was so hard it could not soak up the rain, and the water that streamed down the rocks in silver cascades helped to fill the ever-deepening pools. Elizabeth kept her shoes on and sheltered under an umbrella when more showers of rain fell, but Mark joined the children, laughing boyishly as he raced knee deep through the water. All the dogs had been taken along and they scampered in and out of the pools, rolling over and over in ecstasy when they found patches of soft mud. Elizabeth had never known wet weather to create such fun, and when they finally returned to the ranch she thought she would never spend a more enjoyable day.

Nature study became even more attractive in the following week. New blades of grass sprang up overnight and soon tiny plants appeared. Elizabeth walked and rode for miles with the children and dogs, watching for opening flowers, and Margaret picked a single bloom from the rarer plants to paint at home. On one of these excursions they came across a group of tourists and they spent an hour together, searching for interesting specimens.

"Some of the tourists told me they met the kids today," said Mark later.

"Yes. They seemed to enjoy it. Especially when Brian showed them some inch ants."

"They were tickled pink. Said it was the best part of the whole trip. They were telling the others all about the dingo tracks they'd seen and everything." Mark rubbed the back of his neck thoughtfully. "You know, I've always tried to keep the kids away from the tourists in case they made a nuisance of themselves. Perhaps that was a mistake."

Meg had become very popular with the tourists. She enjoyed meeting people and often played her guitar for them. The rest of the staff began to join in the social evenings, usually finishing in the kitchen with a pot of tea when the tourists retired to bed. Elizabeth was often the first to break away, for she still tired before midnight and worried about not being fresh for work.

"Time for me to leave you," she said one night, rinsing her cup and saucer at the sink. "Don't talk about me when I've gone."

"No sense in it then," laughed Noreen. "It's no fun when you can't see the effects."

Scattered clouds had lingered for a time after the rain, but now the sky was clear and the stars shone in all their glory. Elizabeth strolled towards the cabins, swinging her torchlight casually as she gave her attention to the beauty of the sky. The sudden piercing pain in her foot made her scream aloud, and when she looked down and saw an ugly creature about six inches long, with a mass of squirming legs, she screamed even harder.

Mark led the way out of the kitchen, closely followed by Noreen and Charles. Elizabeth's torch had fallen to the ground, but it was still shining and they raced towards it. They found Elizabeth leaning up against the wall of an empty cabin, holding her foot with both hands.

"Was it a snake?" demanded Mark.

"No."

"Are you sure?"

"It was a smaller thing. Kind of greeny-brown with lots of legs," gasped Elizabeth. "I saw it. I'm sure."

"A centipede," said Charles.

"Look around and see if you can see it, Noreen. Charles, run down to Rose and ask her to come up. We'll be at the house." Mark slipped an arm behind Elizabeth's shoulders, feeling her stiffen instantly. "Relax, Elizabeth. If you're sure it wasn't a snake you've nothing to worry about. I'm going to carry you over to the house."

He scooped her up and Elizabeth allowed her head to droop onto his shoulder. She felt cold, but beads of sweat had broken out on her body and now she was beginning to shake. Noreen caught them up near the bungalow.

"It was a centipede all right. I found it just before it reached the edge of the grass."

"That's a relief. You'd better blow the whistle for the doctor, Noreen. Rose is sure to want to talk to him."

Noreen went into the schoolroom while Mark carried Elizabeth into the sitting-room. He kicked some magazines off the settee, then lowered her gently and sat beside her. He kept his arm around her and Elizabeth made no attempt to move away. Her head was swimming, her leg was throbbing and she needed all the support he could give. Despite his repeated assurances that she would be all right she could sense his deep concern and knew that he was fighting down his own agitation.

Noreen was still blowing the two tones on the special whistle that set off the alarm at the radio station outside operating hours, when Mrs. Chapman arrived with a jug of ice cubes. She found a plastic bucket, tipped the ice cubes in and added cold water, then carried it to the sitting-room.

"Here you are, Elizabeth, put your foot in this. It'll go numb and take the pain away."

Elizabeth began to lose touch with reality. Somebody wrapped something warm about her shoulders and she vaguely heard the sound of a vehicle. She even thought she heard Brian and Margaret, then Rose's face loomed up before her.

"Elizabeth, pay attention," said Rose sternly. "Do you take any kind of medicine?"

Elizabeth shook her head weakly. "No."

"No sleeping tablets, no tonics or anything?"

"No, I haven't had any for months."

"Good." Rose went into the schoolroom to talk to the doctor by radio. They discussed the case for several minutes, then Rose came back to her patient.

"Is your Doctor's box up to date, Mark?"

"Yes, we've got plenty of everything."

"Good. The doctor says I can give her a sedative. We can call back if she develops any serious symptoms. Otherwise we'll just check with the medical session in the morning."

Rose insisted that she must stay to keep an eye on Elizabeth. She had only guessed most of her patient's medical history, but she was fairly certain that her diagnosis was along the right lines and was worried in case the shock caused a relapse into her former nervous disorder. Mark was just as adamant that he would be unable to rest. Mrs. Chapman and Noreen remade his bed, then Elizabeth was laid in it, already half asleep, and Rose and Mark were left to watch over her.

CHAPTER EIGHTEEN

ELIZABETH BECAME very restless when the sedative began to wear off. The pain reminded her of incidents she had wanted to forget for ever, and when she opened her eyes occasionally she did not recognise her surroundings or any of the people.

She awakened properly at last to find herself in a strange bed, in a strange room. Mark was sitting on a wooden chair beside her, holding her hand.

"Oh dear," she said. She blushed but did not withdraw her hand. She could remember some of the things that had happened last night and how much comfort he had brought to her.

"How are you feeling now?" he asked.

"Much better, thank you." Elizabeth raised her head and saw the strange hump in the bed, just about where her feet should be. "What on earth is that?"

"It's a box to keep the bedclothes off your sore foot."

"Did you make it?"

"As a matter of fact I did." Now it was Mark's turn to blush. "Don't worry, Rose has been here all night. She's just mixing another concoction. She said you would be awake soon."

195

Elizabeth lay back and studied him for a moment. His hair was ruffled, his eyes were puffy and shadowed and bristles were sprouting around his chin.

"I suppose I'm in your bed," she said. "Didn't you get any sleep at all?"

"I couldn't have settled down anywhere. I was too worried."

Rose came in at that moment, sparing Elizabeth the effort of continuing the conversation. She also looked tired, but she spoke as briskly and efficiently as ever.

"So you're awake. You don't look so bad, considering everything." She felt Elizabeth's pulse and nodded as though satisfied. "I don't think we're going to have any complications."

"It was my own fault," said Elizabeth. "I shouldn't have gone out at night wearing sandals. Steve warned me about that, the very first day."

"Well, we all do the same silly things. Risky, I suppose, but there you are. Who can be bothered to keep changing shoes?"

"It's getting a bit late in the year for centipedes and so on," said Mark. "The rain's brought them out."

"Well, no need for you to hang about now," Rose told him. "I'm going to give Elizabeth the once-over. You'll probably just catch the end of the medical session. You can tell the doctor she's awake."

Rose instructed Elizabeth to stay in bed and she

made no attempt to argue. Her foot was still throbbing and spasmodic fierce pains shot up her leg. In addition she felt weak and shaky. She had no inclination to read and did not sit up for long. Mark called in often during the day and Noreen brought her meals across.

"Gee, you caused a commotion," joked Noreen. "Bill and Lesley heard you shriek right across at the homestead. They thought it was a rain bird."

"What's that supposed to be?"

"A bird. I forget its real name, but it sets up an awful racket when there's rain about. It sounds like a woman being murdered."

"I suppose I must have upset the tourists, too."

"They didn't know what was going on. We'd all disappeared by the time they got out of bed. One fellow reckoned it was a dingo howling."

Mrs. Chapman visited her the following afternoon, bringing the battery lamp with her. "Here you are, my dear. Keep this until you feel better, just in case you want to read or anything in the night."

"Thank you. I told Mark he needn't keep the power on just for me, but he wouldn't switch it off."

"No, I suppose not. There's nothing like having a light at night when you're not feeling well."

Mrs. Chapman went on to tell her what everybody had been doing during the past two days. Elizabeth already knew that Mark and the children had moved into tourists cabins and Rose had moved into the bungalow with the baby, but she was surprised to hear that Mark had prevented visits by other members of the staff.

"He reckoned that Rose, Noreen and himself were sufficient to begin with," explained Mrs. Chapman. "You couldn't get proper rest if folks were trailing in and out of here all day."

"I see." Elizabeth lay quietly for a moment, thinking back over recent events. "Mrs. Chapman, why has Mark been so perturbed over this? He seems to have turned the whole place upside down. Surely people have been bitten by things before."

"He thinks a lot of you."

"But there's more to it than that. I mean, when it happened, when he brought me over here, I could tell he was in a state and he was as white as a sheet. I remember thinking, just before I went so dizzy, he'd be needing Rose's help next."

"Yes, it gave him a severe shock." Mrs. Chapman looked at her pensively. "I know Mark doesn't like to talk about it, but I don't think there's any harm in telling you." There was another maddening pause. "Mark's wife was bitten by a snake. A King Brown."

"By a snake!" gasped Elizabeth. "Is that how she died?"

"Yes."

"No wonder he hates snakes so much."

"The poison didn't kill her. Apparently she had a weak heart and the shock was too much for her. She was dead before they got through to the doctor." Mrs. Chapman sighed. "Poor Mark didn't know whether to carry on here or not. He blamed himself for bringing her to live here, because he knew she was nervous. Nobody knew about her heart, though."

"There always seemed to be a bit of a mystery about her death," said Elizabeth.

"Yes. Well, a story about someone dying from snake bite would have ruined the tourist trade. The cause of death was given as heart failure. True enough, but Mark always felt guilty about it."

"I see."

"I was one who persuaded him to stay. I told him he owed it to his wife after all the work she'd put into this place, getting it started." Mrs. Chapman sat still for a few seconds, then gave a little nervous cough and leaned forward again. "Elizabeth, you do like Mark, don't you?"

"Of course."

"Well, why don't you give him a bit of encouragement?" Elizabeth looked up startled, and the other woman pressed on while she still had the nerve. "You'd be good for each other, Elizabeth. He's very fond of you, and he's already hinted that he's ready for marriage again. Why don't you help him a bit? It should be easier now you know why he feels so guilty about the past."

"He had you in mind when he talked about marriage."

"Me?" Mrs. Chapman's solemn expression suddenly dissolved and she shook with laughter.

"Me? Marry again? Not on your life. I'm not the marrying type, my dear, and Mark knows it better than anyone. I can't stand being in one place longer than a few months. That's why I only come here for the winter season. I wouldn't have married Jeff if he hadn't been a travelling worker who'd take me with him."

"Oh dear," sighed Elizabeth.

Mrs. Chapman recovered from her amusement and leaned forward again. "You don't seem to have a very high opinion of yourself. First you think Mark's interested in Olive — then me. It must be obvious to everybody else that he's keen on you."

Mrs. Chapman went soon afterwards, leaving Elizabeth's thoughts in turmoil. She felt that she would never be able to face Mark again after the cook's disclosures, but her embarrassment faded into sympathy as she thought of the tragedy of his wife's death. She could understand the battles he had fought with himself, trying to come to a decision about giving up the ranch, and remembered what he had told her about riding out to look at the scenery whenever he was in doubt.

The next day Elizabeth felt well enough to return to her cabin. Her foot was still stiff and painful, but she hobbled across with Charles giving her a helping hand. The children had apparently been given permission to visit her, and they brought a large jar filled with wild flowers.

"Thank you, they're lovely," said Elizabeth. "Did

you arrange them, Margaret?"

"Everybody collected them, but I put them in the vase."

"It's very artistic. Thank you very much."

She had felt shy about meeting Mark again, but as the day wore on and he did not come she began to miss him. At about four o'clock a tap came on the door and the familiar voice called to her.

"It's Mark. Can I come in?"

"Yes of course."

Mark opened the door carefully, balancing a tray on one hand. He paused there for a moment, looking at Elizabeth in her easy chair. Rufus was sprawled at her feet, his head lifted to inspect the latest arrival and his tail thumping a welcome.

"Tea time," said Mark brightly. "Mrs. Chapman has made some little iced cakes specially."

"How nice of you. You can put the tray down on the stool. I'm not using it for my feet at the moment."

"How are you feeling now?"

"Very well, thank you. I'm sorry about all the fuss I've caused."

Mark set the tray down and dragged the upright chair closer to her. "You don't need to be sorry. It's made everybody realise how much they appreciate you." There was an awkward pause and he bent forward, resting his forearms on his knees. "You know, Elizabeth, I think an awful lot of you, but I just couldn't pluck up enough courage to say so before. For one thing, I wasn't sure how you'd take it. You always seem so scared of affection."

"I'm sorry. But I am."

"Well this time I just have to say something. It was terrible the other night. It was just like history repeating itself all over again." Mark occupied himself by pouring out the tea. He put the teapot down and looked at her again. "You know, my wife died after being bitten. It happened to be a snake, but a centipede might have had the same effect. Not that we'll ever know."

"Mrs. Chapman told me a little about it," said Elizabeth.

"I didn't report the snake bite. I let it be passed off as ordinary heart failure."

"It wouldn't have made any difference if you had reported it."

"You don't think I did wrong? I was thinking of the tourist trade. About the effect on business."

"If you hadn't been near at the time you wouldn't have known, would you? And telling about it wouldn't have brought her back."

"No." Mark shook his head sorrowfully and clenched his hands. "When that happened the other night I was scared to death. I thought I was going to lose the only other person who's meant anything to me ever since. Rose kept saying she was sure your heart was strong, but all I could think was she could easily be mistaken. And you had been so ill before you came here. That's why Rose was taking so many precautions."

Mark waited, but Elizabeth refused to meet his gaze.

"Look, Elizabeth, you must have realised by now how much I think of you. I love you, Elizabeth. I want to marry you when you're ready." She made no answer and he caught hold of her hand. "Elizabeth, say something, please. I love you."

Elizabeth pulled her hand gently away. "You know nothing about me. You can't love someone you don't know."

"I know enough to satisfy me. You don't have to tell me any more unless you want to. Sometimes it helps. I know I should have talked to someone sooner."

Elizabeth shook her head. "I don't think I can. And you can't marry a person if you know nothing about their background."

Mark took her hand again and she allowed it to rest in his. "Elizabeth, you needn't be afraid. You won't shock me. I know you've been very badly hurt and let down by a man called Jack." She jerked her head round and stared at him in alarm, and he patted her hand gently. "You kept saying his name when you were feeling so crook the other night. I suppose he was the villain in the piece. And Rose is sure you've had a baby." Elizabeth tensed and he hastened to add, "She wasn't just gossiping about you. You must believe that. She was trying to explain why you always seem so — er — distrustful."

203

Elizabeth nodded, her eyes filling with tears. "She was right. A little girl."

"What happened to her? Has she been adopted?"

"No." The tears welled over and trickled unheeded down her cheeks. "She was nearly two years old when the accident happened. I kept hold of her, but she was killed."

"My poor dear. I'm sorry."

Elizabeth gulped. "I was expecting another child, but I lost that one too. I suppose it was just as well."

Mark could not restrain his next question. "What happened to the father? That was Jack, I suppose?"

Elizabeth stared unseeingly into space. "He died, too. It was mostly his fault. He was the one who started passing bottles around. He often drank too much. It was too crowded and a stove got knocked over. They were cooking fish on the deck. I think I said once it happened in Greece." She finally looked at Mark, determined to tell him everything. "I thought we were married. I thought we were a happy family. But afterwards, after all the fire and the operations and the deaths and everything, I found out that we weren't married at all. He was already married to somebody else."

"Oh, Elizabeth!" Mark slipped his arms around her and held her close. "Elizabeth! You poor darling. No wonder you thought you'd never trust a man again."

Elizabeth lay in his arms weeping softly. She felt comforted by his embrace and knew that her tears were healthy ones this time, not tears of a nervous breakdown that would go on and on until she was exhausted. Gradually she gained control over her sobs. She fumbled for a handkerchief and Mark allowed her to move away and sit upright again. She blew her nose and managed a smile.

"Oh, look! We let the tea go cold," she exclaimed.

Mark smiled. "I hope that's the worst of our problems from now on. Let's make a fresh start. We've both been haunted by memories. Let's try to push the past away — far back where it belongs." He swept the blond lock of hair from his brow with the sweeping gesture she had come to know so well. "Elizabeth, don't you think you could learn to love me as much as I love you? You know I'm free — that there's nobody else. And you said you feel at home here."

Elizabeth nodded. "I would hate to leave."

"What about the children? Do you think you could face the job of taking on five children?"

Elizabeth looked at the bunch of wild flowers in a jar decorated with coloured paper, and thought of the children. Margaret, who needed to feel wanted, Brian who needed a boost to his self-confidence, Julie who was still so shy she scarcely said a word, and Carl and Pauline — both full of fun and enthusiastic about anything new.

"Yes," she said. "Yes. I love those children."

"And you could learn to love me, too?"

Elizabeth looked into his eyes — those grey eyes

that were sometimes stern, sometimes twinkling with amusement, and now full of yearning.

"Yes," she answered. "Yes, I think I could do that, too."